ORPHAN IN THE BLUE SATIN DRESS

VICTORIAN ROMANCE

JESSICA WEIR

PUREREAD.COM

Copyright © 2025 PureRead Ltd

www.pureread.com

All rights reserved. No part of this publication may be reproduced, distributed or transmitted in any form or by any means, without prior written permission.

Publisher's Note: This is a work of fiction. Names, characters, places, and incidents are a product of the author's imagination. Locales and public names are sometimes used for atmospheric purposes. Any resemblance to actual people, living or dead, or to businesses, companies, events, institutions, or locales is completely coincidental.

CONTENTS

Dear reader, get ready for another great story…	1
Chapter 1	3
Chapter 2	13
Chapter 3	22
Chapter 4	36
Chapter 5	54
Chapter 6	71
Chapter 7	82
Chapter 8	90
Chapter 9	99
Chapter 10	105
Chapter 11	115
Chapter 12	122
Chapter 13	131
Chapter 14	137
Chapter 15	143
Chapter 16	153
Chapter 17	160
Chapter 18	169
Chapter 19	181
Chapter 20	188
Other Books By Jess Weir	203
Our Gift To You	205

DEAR READER, GET READY FOR ANOTHER GREAT STORY...

A VICTORIAN ROMANCE

Turn the page and let's begin

CHAPTER 1

"**B**lessed are the poor in spirit, for theirs is the Kingdom of Heaven." The sign had been on the wall of the schoolroom for as long as Violet Marsh could remember. She could read well, even though she had never been taught to write, and still, the saying made no sense to her.

She was surely poor in spirit, for what pauper in the Lambeth Workhouse was not? But the Kingdom of Heaven? How was that her's, or Joe's, or anybody's but those who were not trapped there with their entire lives being lived out on Renfrew Road?

"What are you staring at now, Violet?" Joe Willis was Violet's only real friend. He was eight years old, just as she was, and she couldn't really remember a time in her life when he hadn't been by her side. Well, except for that one distant memory.

"That sign. It doesn't make sense."

"Well, I can read it. Maybe I'm the clever one," Joe said and began to chuckle; he was a teaser and a joker, a bright light in a very dark space.

"I can read it, too, silly!" Violet said and stifled her own laughter, not wanting the Mistress to hear her and punish her. They were supposed to be reading a page from an old newspaper, a page they would be asked questions about in a few minutes. "I mean, it just doesn't make sense. How is the Kingdom of Heaven mine, or yours, for that matter? Look at us all, Joe. We must be the poor in spirit, but the Kingdom of Heaven is nowhere to be seen."

"Take that sort of nonsense with a pinch of salt," he said with an eight-year-old's air of knowledge. "The Kingdom of Heaven ain't really meant for the likes of us. It's meant for those as can afford it. The fine folks who dress nice for church on a Sunday."

"How are *they* poor in spirit?"

"Because they're too mean to care about anybody else." He took so long to answer that Violet knew he was making it up as he went along. She didn't mind, of course, because whether he made things up or not, Joe Willis always made her feel better. "They're saving all their spare coins in case St Peter charges at the gate."

"Stop it, I'll start laughing, and Mistress Packham will

punish me. Have you read the newspaper properly? She'll be asking us in a moment."

"Yes, it's all in here!" he said and tapped the side of his head. He pulled a face, and Violet had to look away this time lest she really started to laugh.

For the children who stayed just a few weeks in the workhouse, the occasional reading lessons had little impact. They would be going back out into the world with their impoverished parents again, and education would be forgotten in the desperate struggle for survival. For those who had spent their lives within the workhouse's walls, the lessons of so many years, albeit they were infrequent, had at least left them with something to show for their miserable existence.

"Never mind, old Vera. Now, there's a woman St Peter would slam the gates shut on," Joe went on, undeterred. "Pinched faced old crow."

Violet bit her tongue. If Vera Packham saw her amusement, she most certainly wouldn't be kind or understanding about it. As far as she was concerned, the poor should be concentrating solemnly on their crime of poverty, not finding reasons to smile. Ever.

She didn't like Violet, but then, she didn't like anybody, most particularly the female inmates of the workhouse. If she saw her smiling, she would either be forced to stand at the front of the little group to be berated and humiliated or worse, sent to see the Master, Micah Turner. He was such a terrifying prospect that the smile was immediately wiped from Violet's face. He wasn't supposed to physically punish the girls and women, nobody was, but she'd heard enough tales from the others to know that he was hardly a man to stick to the regulations unless it suited his purposes to do so. So, Violet decided to concentrate, giving the Mistress her fullest attention and her best answers when she was quizzed about the contents of the newspaper page.

Sooner or later, Violet would spend more time under the watchful gaze of Vera Packham. Vera was the Mistress of the workhouse, but she spent a good deal of time overseeing the category of inmates known as *girls*. Girls were aged between eight and fifteen years and were finally separated from the boys. Currently, Violet and Joe were simply classed as *children*, and whilst their dormitories were separate, their daily activities were not. They were slowly but surely being made ready for long days of work, anything from ten to twelve hours with nothing but sleep at the end to recommend it.

Violet knew a little more about what went on in the other parts of the workhouse because Joe's mother was also an inmate. Cruelly separated from her son, as all mothers were, Ida Willis had a weekly meeting with Joe in the big room. It was a meeting commonly referred to as an interview, something Violet thought rather formal for an hour spent with a relation.

Joe knew what sort of work they would be doing when they moved up in category from child to boy and girl, respectively. He never held anything back, but he always told her that they would survive it. It had felt much more believable in the days when their imminent separation was so far away it was almost not real. Now, however, when they might be torn apart any given day, Violet wondered if she really could survive it.

If only she could have an interview once a week with Joe, but she knew the Master would never allow it. They weren't family, after all. There would be no interview for Violet in the big room, not with anybody. With no mother, father, or siblings, and without Joe Willis, Violet would be truly alone in the world. She would have given anything to have a mother, even one she could only see for an hour a week. It would be somebody to hold in her heart and look forward to seeing.

As it was, all she had was a pale memory, so opaque that it could hardly be trusted.

Violet was sweeping the floor of the dormitories in the children's block when Joe came looking for her. He was smiling, as always, but the skin around his eyes looked red and blotchy, she knew he'd been crying. He'd just spent an hour with his mother in the big room, and he was always a little down afterwards, even if he tried to hide it. But this time was different, he never normally cried.

"Joe, how's your ma?" Violet asked, pausing in her sweeping but careful to keep an eye on the door in case the Mistress or one of the nurses appeared.

"She's all right. She's... well..."

"Joe?" she said when his eyes looked glassy with welling tears.

"She's losing her marbles," he whispered as he blinked back his tears.

"How? What do you mean?" she whispered back.

"She's saying all sorts of funny things, things that ain't making no sense. She keeps talking about Grandma, but she's been dead donkeys' years. I never even met my Grandma, but Ma keeps talking as if she's in the next room. She kept saying, *go into the back room and see your Grandma, she'll give you a penny*. I tried to keep her quiet. I didn't want none of the others realising she was going funny."

"But shouldn't you say something? Shouldn't somebody be helping her?"

"Are you in the same workhouse as me? They'd stick her in the funny farm at Couldson." He was exasperated, but still kindly.

"Couldson?" She'd heard of it in passing and wished she knew what it was, for asking him seemed to cause yet more pain.

"That's where the Cane Hill Asylum is, Vi. Couldson. It's near Croydon, I think."

"I don't know where Croydon is. Is it nearby?"

"For someone on foot, it might just as well be Timbuktu!"

"That's a long way away. No wonder you want to keep it quiet. Maybe she'll perk up next week. She might just not be well this week. She might have a stomach upset that's making her feel a bit peculiar."

"Yes, that'll be it!" Joe brightened, but Violet could see it was forced. He was clutching at straws, snagging any little hope which floated by.

Violet wasn't so sure that her own theory would cut the mustard. She'd heard enough tales of the men and women in the workhouse going *'round the bend*, as it was known, losing their minds to the soul-destroying grind and heartache of the workhouse. Separated from children, never knowing when they might be leaving that awful place, it all took its toll. Violet knew by instinct that the workhouse was a harder place for those who had reached full maturity. That was when the Master and Mistress, not to mention the unfeeling wardens, could forget all ideas of protection. A person spending their life in the workhouse would have to be old and infirm before they could hope for any kindness or respite. And even then, kindness was always a commodity in short supply.

"She'll be all right, Joe," Violet said and patted her friend on the shoulder in a display of childlike caring.

"Yes, she'll be all right. I suppose I better make myself scarce before the old crow turns up and catches me here." He grinned, relieved to have been so easily fooled by Violet, and, more importantly, by himself.

As she continued to sweep, Violet felt so terribly sorry for Joe. He loved his mother, even though he'd only seen her for an hour a week, year after year. She'd brought Joe into the workhouse when he was just a baby, shortly after his father had died. His mother, without any family to speak of, had been unable to manage. The landlords were charging too much rent, and the businessmen were paying workers too little. For families where there was no father, life was impossible.

For the first time, Violet felt relieved not to have a family member to worry about. She just knew that Joe was suffering terribly, his worries gnawing away at his good little soul. That feeling of helplessness invading his every moment. If Violet had a mother and she was suffering the way Joe's mother was, how would she manage? In her almost loveless life, did she really have the better deal?

Of course, Violet knew she didn't. She longed for a mother, so much so that she knew her old memories couldn't be trusted. Nonetheless, she played that little snatch of memory in her mind over and over again, keeping it fresh and alive regardless of whether it was real life or fiction.

Leaning on her broom, Violet closed her eyes for a moment and drew the oft remembered memory to mind. She couldn't see herself, as such, for the memory was taking place through her own eyes. However, she could look down at herself, a tiny girl of no more than two or three, wearing a pretty blue dress with a cream bow. The colour so bright it was vibrant and something she could never imagine owning, let alone wearing, but there it was in her memory. She looked down at her feet and could see the toes of neat little black boots that popped out from beneath the hem of the pretty dress with every step she took.

Her arm reached up, and her hand grasped that of a woman. She couldn't see the woman's face, but she was sure the woman was young, warm, and kind. Violet didn't know how she knew it, but in her memory, she knew that the woman loved her so much. It was the very thing which made her believe that the woman was her mother.

The scenery was always the same, with soft green grass neatly clipped, trees whose leaves rustled in the breeze. There was water, she could see it, like a big pond that drew her eye. Then the lady urged her to keep moving, and they crossed a wide road to another park on the other side. Violet turned her head, her mouth falling open as she looked down the wide road and saw a huge house in the distance, so big it was like a fine palace. But the lady kept her moving, and she heard her laughing at the childish wonder. As they head into the greenery once more, the wonderful memory comes to an end.

Had it really happened? And if it had, was the young woman her mother? Violet felt certain she would never know; certain in a way which made her heart sink and her eyes well with tears. She felt sorry for Joe, and she felt sorry for herself. What would she do without him when they were separated? Who would she tell the strange little memory to? Everybody else she'd told had simply laughed at her.

Vera Packham, when Violet had asked about her mother, had just laughed. She said she could hardly remember when Violet had arrived in the workhouse but that, like most orphans, she had probably been born into sin and abandoned at the gates by her prostitute of a mother. When Violet had told her of the pretty blue dress with the cream bow, the Mistress had thrown her head back and laughed cruelly. From that day, Violet had stopped telling the story of her memory. Even the other children had laughed at her. All except for Joe, of course.

Once again, she wondered how she was going to manage without him. Violet couldn't help but throw another small prayer up to God. It wasn't fancy or worded in any particular impressive way like the one's in mass, but it came from her heart. "Keep Joe safe…"

CHAPTER 2

It was after morning prayers and breakfast that the Master of the workhouse, Micah Turner, strode into the dining hall. Whispering a few words into the ear of one of the wardens, he kept his eyes on the children the whole time. Standing at the front of the dining hall, he waited patiently for the men, women, and older girls and boys to leave the children sitting at the front two tables alone.

The long trestle tables stretched right across the hall, lined up from the front to the back of the room. Everyone faced forward, no one was permitted to sit opposite anybody else. Conversation was not encouraged, for the rules of the workhouse stated that a pauper in receipt of such welfare must be quiet in order to appreciate what they were given. As far back as Violet could remember, the only sounds to generally issue forth in that room were spoons scraping on plates.

Occasionally, there was an outburst of some sort when some poor person had become suddenly disturbed or mentally infirm, but even on such occasions, all eyes remained facing front.

Violet wanted to look for Joe, but that would have meant looking behind her to the row of little boys. If Micah Turner saw her do that, she certainly would be in trouble. Instead, with her breakfast of watery gruel washing about in her stomach, she sat nervously awaiting what she was sure would be coming. This was the day they were to be separated.

"Eyes front, all of you," the Master said when the hall was finally cleared of everybody but the children. "Now then, some of you here today have reached the age where you might successfully be moved into other blocks here in the workhouse. I speak, of course, of those of you who have reached the age of eight years. There are five of you here today, so step forward and stand before me. The rest of you may leave."

The children, all afraid of Micah, began to move immediately, nobody speaking a word. Violet and Joe stood at the front fearfully with the other three children, all of whom were boys. Wherever she was going next in life, it was to be alone in the company of complete strangers without a single familiar face barring that of the awful mistress. Tears pressed at the back of her eyes, but Violet knew she must hide them, so she quickly swallowed down the emotion.

Violet couldn't see Joe, but she could sense him standing next to her. She wanted to look at him, to take in the sight of his face at close quarters one last time. They would still eat in the same hall, but he would be away from her, with the boys, and she would find herself in trouble for seeking him out and staring at him. Of all the cruelty she had seen, and all the deprivations she had suffered, having Joe taken from her was the worst of them. It hadn't happened yet, and already it was more than she could bear.

"You are to move to your new blocks tomorrow after prayers and breakfast. Violet Marsh, you will be taken by the Mistress to the girls' dormitory block and given your new clothing, for which you are expected to be grateful." He pierced her with his black-eyed stare.

Violet lowered her own eyes and gently nodded, unable to look at him for fear.

"And you boys will, of course, be set up in the boys' dormitory with your new clothes." He paused and strode slowly up and down the line of terrified little children, peering down at them, his face creased as if they offended him. "All of you, whatever your sex, will now find yourselves gainfully employed from morning until night. Your lessons will now end, for you have been given enough instruction in the art of reading. From now on, you will be learning how to fit into the world beyond the workhouse, for I expect you all to work hard and apply yourselves so that you will be ready to go out into the world and stand on your own two feet for a change, instead of forever relying on charity and the kindness of others."

Although he seemed to believe what he was saying, there was nothing about her time in the Lambeth Workhouse, which spoke to Violet of either charity or kindness. Perhaps those words had different meanings within these walls.

"Learn from the mistakes of your parents. Don't allow yourselves to be as weak as they have been, as sinful as they have been," he went on.

Violet felt Joe stir beside her.

"Stand still, boy! You fidget like that good-for-nothing mother of yours. Not losing your mind, too, are you?"

"Don't you speak about her that way!" Joe roared, utterly furious. "It's *your* cruelty which brings her down! You did this! You all did this!"

"Come here, boy!" Micah Turner's roar was far louder than anything which could hope to issue forth from Joe's eight-year-old lungs. "This minute!"

"You talk about charity and kindness, and you don't even know what it means. You act as if you're not sinful because you're not poor like my ma, but you're wrong. It's how you treat others, which makes you good or bad, not how much money you have!" Joe was not about to give up.

Violet began to shake. Her dear little friend was going to suffer for his outburst, she knew he was.

When Joe stood his ground, Micah strode forward and seized him roughly by his collars. It was so rough that Violet heard the fabric tear, and Joe was dragged along on his toes, almost lifted from the ground. He was thrown face-forward across the trestle table at which Violet had just been eating, scattering wooden bowls everywhere, and his trousers hastily dragged down.

"Birch!" Micah bellowed at one of the waiting wardens. "Now!" The warden scampered away.

Violet felt tears in her eyes. Joe was going to be beaten, and Micah Turner was so angry that the beating would be a harsh one. Her heart was pounding, and when the warden raced back into the dining hall carrying Micah Turner's birch cane, she was almost sick. She had to swallow hard; if she was sick now, she would be punished too, female or not, Micah would not stick to the true regulations of the Workhouse.

Micah raised his arm high above his head, the cane held aloft as if he were a swordsman running into battle.

Violet wanted to look away, but that would be to leave Joe to suffer alone. She forced herself to look, to keep her eyes open, and she prayed that the beating wouldn't be harsh.

However, the cane was brought down so fast that it cut through the air, making an awful swishing sound before the loud crack of it finally connected with Joe's skin. Joe cried out loudly and didn't stop as Micah brought the cane down over and over and over. Joe was screaming in pain, and Violet could no longer hear the swish and crack of the birch cane over his cries. She was walking on the spot, her feet wanting to propel her across the short distance to help her friend, but her fear was holding her back, and she felt powerless and small.

Micah continued to raise the cane and seemed to bring it down harder and harder each time, showing no sign of tiring. When Violet saw a great tide of blood fly from the cane, she realised that the beating had been ferocious enough to break Joe's skin. The warden looked distinctly uncomfortable, and Violet knew that the man knew this was wrong. However, as Micah continued with no let up, the man did nothing.

Finally, Violet ran out and tugged at Micah Turner's trouser leg.

"Stop, please stop! You're killing him!" Violet was crying and shaking, but she was determined.

Micah's arm stopped in mid-air before he turned to look down at her. Black eyes full of hatred glared at her. Violet froze on the spot, she had never been so terrified in her life. When he brought the cane back down, she thought it was over. Violet let go of Micah's trouser leg and stood trembling before him. Without warning, Micah Turner swiped her hard across the face with the bloodied cane.

The pain was searing, and the shock so great that Violet fell back.

She could hear the whimpering of the three boys who stoically stayed where they had been left, a little line of trembling, terrified children. She wanted to raise her hand to her face, but she was too afraid that her cheek would be rent apart, a wide gash disfiguring her.

Violet looked up at Micah, he seemed to be in something of a trance. Staring down at her as if he couldn't quite imagine how she'd ended up on the floor. He looked like a man possessed, and Violet held her breath, wondering what was coming next.

"Get them out of my sight," Micah said when he finally came back to himself. "Get their nurse to attend to them and see that they have nothing else to eat until breakfast tomorrow. That will perhaps teach them to know their place in this world." And with that, the Master strode out of the dining hall, the bloodied cane swinging at his side.

Later that day, whilst the rest of the children were sitting down with the other workhouse inmates to eat their meagre evening meal, Violet and Joe were left in the children's block with one of the nurses. She had patched up Joe's injuries, although she had been ordered not to send the boy to the infirmary. Micah Turner was determined that the insolent child would work his first day in the boys' block from one end to the other, no lazing about in a comfortable bed in the infirmary being waited on hand and foot.

"Does it still hurt?" Violet asked as Joe lay on the scrubbed wooden floor on his stomach.

"Yes, but it's not so bad. I wouldn't take it back, Vi, that rotter deserved to hear what he really is. Nobody says things like that about my ma, nobody!" He was vehement, and she believed him. Joe Willis was nothing if not loyal, and Violet was honoured to have him as a friend. Her best friend. Her only friend.

Her own face was, in the end, not split apart, but there was a red welt that had already begun to bruise. Luckily, her face wouldn't be scarred forever, not like Joe's tortured behind. Oh, how she despised Micah Turner. If she had the power to kill him, she would do it.

"Your ma would be so proud of you, Joe, the way you stood up for her and everything."

"And she'd clout me and all, for being so stupid too," he said and chuckled. "She's always telling me to keep my cheeky gob shut, or I'll get myself in trouble."

"But you weren't cheeky this time, you were right. The Master is to blame, they all are. Even the ones who seem kinder just stand there and gawp when they should be helping." Violet pictured the warden who had stood by and despised him for his cowardice. They were children, for goodness sake!

"I know," Joe said sadly.

"And now we're going to be split up, and I'll never see you again," Violet said and suddenly sobbed; today was more than little Violet could take.

"You'll see me in the dinner hall," Joe said, and from his prone position, he reached for her hand. "You just look for me at every meal, and I'll be there. And don't forget, we ain't going to be in this place forever. As soon as I'm old enough to get a job that'll support Ma, I'll be out of here, and you're coming with me." His eyes shone as they always did when he was telling a wild tale.

"Do you promise?" Violet asked, trying to swallow down her heartbreak. "You won't leave me here?"

"I'd never, ever leave you here. We'll leave this place together, sticking our tongues out at old Micah Turner on the way out!" he went on and began to laugh as he demonstrated just how he would perform the parting gesture.

"Joe, what will I do without you?" Violet asked, her tears turning to laughter as Joe continued to put on his cheeky performance.

"You'll survive, Vi. We both will, you mark my words. One day we'll look back on this and know we made it out. I promise."

CHAPTER 3

As they filed out of the chapel the next morning after prayers, Joe came up beside Violet and sneakily squeezed her hand. He clearly knew that she was struggling not to cry, for this was the day they were to be parted, each sent to their own block, only ever to see one another from afar.

Violet squeezed his hand back, but they quickly let go of one another, knowing just how much more they would be punished if they were seen. Comfort between human beings wasn't something that paupers in the workhouse could afford.

When they were seated in the dining hall, Violet could hardly swallow down the watery gruel, but she tried to ladle it into her mouth from the small, hard wooden bowl. She knew, of course, that to leave it would be remarked upon; she would be lambasted as an ingrate, the worst thing she could be when in receipt of such charity. So, with her throat hardly agreeing to swallow, she made her way through the awful meal.

She didn't know what the rest of the day would bring, but she wasn't so afraid of that as she was heartbroken by the knowledge that she and her only friend were to be torn away from one another. If only she could claim him for a brother and beg for an interview once a week in the big room. But everybody knew that she was an orphan, that she had no relations in all the world, at least none who would lay claim to her, at any rate.

When she was finally taken from the dining hall to the girls' block by the Mistress, Vera Packham, Violet was, of course, the only girl. She was the only one of age, with no familiar face to settle her into her new surroundings. It all seemed to happen so fast, and Vera Packham had carted her away so quickly that she hadn't even had a final look at Joe before leaving the hall.

"Firstly, we shall get your new clothes, Marsh," the Mistress said, with not even enough warmth in her soul to address Violet by her first name.

Violet said nothing, she merely nodded and tried to keep step with Vera, who seemed to march everywhere at great speed. Vera was tall and lean, her legs so long that Violet was almost running to keep up with her. There was something rather masculine about Vera Packham, with her square jaw and long nose. Her dark hair was pulled back sharply off her face and wound into a tight, severe bun at the back of her head. She had only a few wiry grey hairs in amongst the darkness, most of which were hidden beneath the soft white cotton cap she always wore.

"Right, in we go," Vera said and roughly pushed Violet ahead of her into a small room. Violet recognised the room, for it was the place in which she had been given her previous outfit, the one she had worn for so long that she had outgrown it. "Right, take off that pinafore and dress and lay them both on the chair," Vera went on with a theatrical grimace. "They will be properly cleaned and checked for lice before they're handed on to the next poor unfortunate."

As far as Violet was concerned, there had been no real need to say such a thing. It served no purpose but to hurt her, to make her feel ashamed, even though she knew that she kept herself and her clothes as clean as possible. What sort of woman found her enjoyment in such spite? Violet could hardly think about the fact that she was going to be almost entirely under the gaze of the Mistress from now on, she took such an interest in the older girls. For a moment, she would have given anything for one of the sharp old nurses or even a warden of so cowardly a nature that they always looked the other way. Vera Packham was, in her own way, almost as frightening as Micah Turner.

"You will need to take everything off, child," Vera said waspishly. "Now!"

"But, Mistress," Violet said, feeling her cheeks burning and her eyes filling with tears.

"Don't *but Mistress* me, child! You are to have everything new; did you not listen to what the Master said yesterday? You are to have a new dress, a new cap, new bloomers, and new stockings. Your boots will have to do since they still fit you, but everything else is to be new. So, you will need to take everything off!"

Violet knew she could do no more than acquiesce as she finally removed everything and stood shivering in that little room. Trying to cover herself, she kept her eyes on the door at all times, her prayers given over entirely to that door never opening while she was in such a state.

However, Vera handed Violet her clothes quickly, and she made short work of dressing herself in the dreadfully long knickers, thick stockings, and shapeless shift dress made of thick and rough cotton fabric, with its design wide stripes. It was all topped off with a cloth cap. It was a uniform, something which would mark her out as a pauper from the workhouse if she was ever seen outside of its walls.

Although Violet could not remember ever living outside of its walls, she had a firm understanding of how the rest of Lambeth saw the inmates of the workhouse. They were looked down on, scorned, even by those who were a hair's breadth from being in the place themselves. The low and the abused always kicked downwards, didn't they?

The striped shift dresses were the same for the girls and women alike. They were marked now, workers of the workhouse. They were apart from the rest of society in a way that they perhaps hadn't quite been as children. As inhabitants of the children's block, they had been taught a little and perhaps even pitied a little, for their circumstances were hardly their own fault. Now, however, Violet had the distinct impression that she was about to start accepting blame for her own situation, as if growing one year older had suddenly made her, at eight years old, entirely responsible for it.

"Good, it fits well enough, but there's still room for growth. Let's just hope you don't grow too quickly, child," Vera said in a far-off voice, which made it seem more as if she were talking to herself rather than Violet. "Well, what do you say?" Focusing again, she turned sharply to look Violet right in the eyes.

"Thank you, Mistress. Thank you for my new clothes," Violet said, knowing full well what was expected of her. The paupers couldn't be given a meal, however meagre, without being almost bent double in gratitude for it. Never mind that most of them broke their backs, working hard for it. That didn't seem to count.

"Of course, the very best way to show your gratitude, child, is to work hard. You are not an infant, you are a girl now, and you will be expected to work like one. The other girls are older, the nearest to your age being ten years old. You will likely remember her; her name is Jeanette. *Jeanette!* she said and shook her head vigorously. "What names these paupers give their children!" Again, she seemed to be speaking to herself.

"Yes, Mistress," Violet said, nodding as vigorously as Vera shook her own head. It was a nod that encompassed all. She was agreeing to work hard, and she was admitting knowledge of Jeanette, a child who had been moved from the children's block and into the girls' block one year before.

"Well, today you are going to learn oakum picking, do you know what that is?"

"Yes, Mistress." Violet stood quietly until she realised that the Mistress' stare meant that she ought to explain. "It's picking apart old pieces of rope, pulling out the strands, so that the oakum can be used in shipbuilding. That is what I've been told, Mistress."

"You have been told correctly. It is perhaps not as easy as it sounds. You will be expected to make a certain weight every day. However, be glad that you were born a female, for were you a male, you would be learning how to crush animal bone and break stones."

"Yes, Mistress," Violet said, and tried to imagine Joe, hardly an inch taller than she was, wielding the sledgehammers that the boys and men used for stone breaking. What a terrible day he was going to have, still carrying the pain and injury of the unnecessary punishment of the day before.

"Come along then, it's time for you to get to work."

Fear was like a living beast within her chest as Violet walked through parts of the workhouse she had never seen before. It pushed down, making it hard to breathe and squeezed her heart until it raced inside like a runaway horse. She knew that the workhouse was big, she just never realised *how big*. Having only ever been kept to the children's block, the chapel, and the dining hall, she was surprised by the length of the corridors, the vastness of the other blocks.

Vera took Violet into a long room lined with benches. Each bench was filled with girls, ranging from the youngest, Jeanette, at ten, to the oldest. The oldest would be fifteen, soon to be moved to the women's block.

The girls barely looked up from their work as Violet was led into the room, although Violet suspected that was more on account of the sudden appearance of the Mistress. Nobody wanted to tempt her annoyance in the girls' block, so it had that much in common with her old accommodation.

In front of each girl was a basket containing the already picked oakum. She could see that some girls clearly worked faster than others, for their baskets were filling faster.

"Millie, as the oldest and the one who is soon to move out of the girls' block, I shall leave it to you to show the newcomer what she is to do," Vera said sharply.

Millie, a girl who would have been pretty had she not been so hard-faced, glared at Violet. Nonetheless, she moved along the bench a little, making room for her to sit down. Without a word, Millie rose, collected another basket, and set it down in front of Violet. She handed her a thick strand of rope, no longer than six inches in length, and finally began to speak.

"You need to work away at the frayed ends, see?" she said in a voice that suggested she had no time for frightened little children. "You pick at it until you can pull out the fibres, strand by strand. When you have a piece like this," she said and pulled a thin fibre from the thick rope, "you throw it into your basket. There, you try."

With little fingers, Violet began to work away at the frayed ends of the rope. Millie had certainly made it look much easier than it was, for it took her several attempts to isolate a single strand, and several attempts more to free it from its nearest neighbours.

"Keep working, girls," Vera Packham said sharply. "I will be back to check up on your progress shortly." And with that, she was gone.

Even before they stopped for their midday bread in the dining hall, Violet's fingers were sore, and one of them was beginning to bleed. She put the rope down on her lap and peered at her fingertips, seeing how the tiniest fragments of fibre had worked their way under her skin to irritate her.

"It's because you've never done a hard day's work in your life, stupid!" Millie said, and the other girls laughed. "Your skin's so soft that the fibres can work their way in so easily. Look at mine," she said and thrust a hand so quickly into Violet's face that Violet shrank back, causing the other girls to laugh again. "See, I've worked so hard that my skin is tough, and the fibres can't get in. Maybe the best way for you to stop it happening is to get a move on, to start pulling your weight."

"I'm trying, but I've never done this before," Violet said, defending herself.

"I'm trying, but I've never done this before," Millie said, mocking her, mimicking her words in an exaggerated whine. "You'd better get used to it, hadn't you? We're not going to carry you on our backs, you're not a child anymore."

"I'm only eight," Violet said and realised that she had never felt younger and smaller than she did at that moment. "I'm sorry, I'm trying to work as fast as I can."

"Then you'd better work harder, hadn't you?" Millie screwed her face up and thrust it towards Violet's face until their noses were almost touching. "Because if you don't make the same pile of oakum as I make by the end of this day, I will beat you. Yes, that's right, I'll *beat* you."

"Millie, she's only little," one of the girls on a bench opposite spoke out.

"I haven't moved away into the women's block yet, Doris!" Millie said, and the girl called Doris looked afraid. "Just you remember why it is you have no front teeth. That's right, Doris!" Millie gave a low, cruel laugh. "There might not be any teeth left for me to knock out now, but I can certainly break your nose."

The room fell to silence. Clearly, all the girls were afraid of Millie. Violet couldn't help but think it ridiculous, for if they stood shoulder to shoulder, Millie's words would be worth nothing. She would be alone, perhaps even afraid of the rest of them. But that was the workhouse. It destroyed nothing faster than a person's spirit.

By the time they had eaten their evening meal and made their way to the girls' dormitory for the night, Violet was bone tired. In some ways, her fear and exhaustion had at least spared her thoughts of Joe and her heartbreak.

Millie hadn't beaten her in the end, and Violet was quick to realise that the girl would undoubtedly be punished if she had done something to the newcomer on her very first day. Violet hadn't picked much more than half the oakum that Millie and the other girls had picked, but at least she still had all her teeth. She wondered if Millie really had knocked Doris' teeth out and quickly concluded that she truly had; Doris had looked so frightened.

She hurriedly put on her nightgown and clambered onto the little hard mattress, Violet was already praying that her stinging fingers would be repaired by morning and that she would easily pick as much oakum as the rest of the girls. Even though the oil lamps were still on full, Violet curled up in her bed and pulled the thin blanket up around her neck, closing her eyes.

"Oh, look, little Violet is already asleep. She's exhausted, bless her cotton socks!" It was unmistakably Millie who was taunting her. "Well, she *has* worked hard, girls, hasn't she?" There came the now familiar titter of laughter, although Violet had already worked out that the laughter came from girls who were too afraid to do anything else. Violet could not think of them as anything other than fools. As the elephant who does not realise, he is stronger than the ringmaster.

"I'm still awake," Violet said sheepishly.

"Well, don't worry, you'll soon be asleep and dreaming the most wonderful dreams, won't you?" Millie said, her voice full of spiteful amusement. "Dreams of walking through the park holding a nice lady's hand. There's soft grass and swaying trees, and you're wearing such a pretty little dress, one that's the most beautiful blue colour." She began to laugh, and the other girls joined in.

Violet moved a little in her bed, looking across the dormitory to where Jeanette sat on her own bed looking greatly chagrined. Her eyes were so apologetic that Violet knew immediately that Jeanette had told the story so that she might curry favour with Millie, the girl she feared the most. But even if Jeanette was afraid, it was a cruel trick. Violet hadn't spoken of that dream for so long, and surely, she could have been no more than five or six years old when she had last mentioned it in front of Jeanette, back when Jeanette was still in the children's block.

"Where is a scruffy little orphan like you to find such a dress, Violet? And where is it now? Did you arrive here in it? Will it be handed back to you when you leave? Oh no, of course it won't, it will be too small."

As Millie continued to taunt her, Violet sank down further beneath her blankets, covering her head.

"Imagine her thinking that she has a mother out there! Well, likely, she does have a mother. Likely that mother got caught out with her in her belly after earning herself a shilling on her back!" Millie went on and shrieked with laughter as one or two of the other girls gasped with surprise. Perhaps they were not all as crude as Millie, after all.

"No, she didn't. Don't you say that, don't you dare say that!" Violet said, realising that she now understood exactly how Joe had felt when he had thrown his safety to one side so that he might defend his precious ma. It didn't matter that Violet didn't know her mother, all that mattered was that she protect her just as Joe, the finest little boy in all the world, had protected his mother.

"Would you listen to her? She'll soon know better than to tell me what to do, won't she, girls?" Millie went on, pausing only to hear general assent from the rest of the group. "Fine words from the daughter of a harlot who dumped her as an unwanted baby on the workhouse steps. The workhouse! She didn't even care enough about you to take you to an orphanage." Millie laughed again, a horrible, cruel laugh.

In the end, Violet put her palms flat over her ears and closed her eyes tightly. She didn't want to hear any more. She couldn't bear the ugly sound of Millie's voice. After a while, the lights went out, and she knew that the room would fall quiet. With one of the wardens sitting just outside the room ready to report on any fooling around, she wouldn't hear a thing out of the dreadful Millie until morning.

And so, Violet Marsh cried herself to sleep. She cried silently, wishing that she had a mother she could see once a week in the big room, and missing Joe Willis more than she could say. Well, at least she might see him in the morning in Chapel or at breakfast. It would only be a glimpse, but that would be enough for her. Just the sight of him would be enough to restore her, to make her stronger, and she vowed to herself to keep going, to remember what he'd said about them leaving there one day, and to never, ever give in.

However, even as she drifted into sleep, Violet wondered if it was just a dream like her dress. She wondered if she had a lifetime of this ahead of her.

CHAPTER 4

Slowly but surely, Joe was getting to grips with his new life in the boys' block. He'd taken a few nasty knocks at first, he'd expected to after all, but they were beginning to like him. Joe was a fast-talking little boy with enough cheek for everybody in the workhouse. However, the truth was that he didn't always feel as bright and breezy as he appeared to be, especially now that he had been separated from Violet. These days, he didn't care quite so much about his audience. It had been easy to feel bright and even fun sometimes when Violet had been around. He'd wanted to make her laugh, to see his little friend smiling once in a great while.

Now, his cheek and foolish behaviour were simply the things that saved him from being bullied by the older boys. They also saved the three young lads who had moved from the children's block with him from being poorly treated, he always included them in his jokes. The little band of four boys had quickly become accepted.

It was a relief, but it was also exhausting. At eight years old, Joe Willis felt like an old man of fifty; bone-tired, his hands calloused from swinging the sledgehammer, his heart aching from missing his friend. There was very little true joy in his fast-talking these days. It was tiring him, even more, to think of ways to make everybody else laugh now that it no longer came to him spontaneously.

"Did you get on all right with your ma the other day, Joe? You looked like you'd been slapped in the face with the door when I saw you." Charlie, one of the older boys, spoke to him quietly as the two of them made their way to the dining hall for their midday bread and water.

"She's not doing so well, Charlie, truth be told. Ah, it's this place, isn't it? Gets to us all in the end," Joe was trying to make light of it, even though he felt he rather trusted Charlie. After all, Charlie had never been one of the boys who had given him the occasional dig when he'd first moved from the children's block.

"It saw my ma off, two years back now," Charlie said conversationally, shaking his head slowly from side to side as he stared into the middle distance. Clearly remembering the mother who had succumbed, no doubt, to one of the many illnesses and deprivations it was possible for a person to succumb to in the Lambeth workhouse.

"I'm sorry to hear that, Charlie. What about your pa?"

"He's still clinging on. That's who I go and see when I'm in the big room for my interview. He's the only family I've got left now."

"And how does he do?"

"He suffers it," Charlie said and chewed his bottom lip.

Charlie was only fourteen years old, and Joe thought he was already beginning to look like a shrunken little old man.

"He was injured before we came in here. He always worked hard, but he did his shoulder in, didn't he? He works as hard as he can with the sledgehammer, but he has to swing the thing with his left arm instead of his right. And you know what they call him for that? That old swine, Micah Turner and his cronies? *Malingerer*. They've actually written that about him, do you know that?"

"Most of them would know a thing or two about real malingering, that's what I reckon. I reckon they know almost as much about malingering as they know about being cruel and spiteful. You never know, though, Charlie, one day we might get our own back, we might, you know?"

"You're one on your own, you are!" Charlie said and started to laugh, although he laughed almost under his breath now that they were almost at the dining hall. "You're a real dreamer!"

"Yeah, why not? A little dreaming never hurt anybody, did it?"

"Maybe the dreaming won't hurt you, Joe, but the disappointment certainly will," Charlie said, and the two boys laughed in a knowing, cynical way. A way that two children ought to know nothing about. Cynicism should be for grown men and women, not them.

Silence reigned as always in the dining hall, with nothing but the occasional soft dull thumps of the tin mugs of water being placed back down on top of the trestle tables. Conversation was not allowed. Neither was twisting and turning in your seat to seek out and make eye contact with your very best friend.

However, Joe generally managed to set eyes on Violet at least once a day, and more often than not, she managed to look back. It always made his little heart swell to see his friend there, and then it made his little heart break to know that he couldn't even speak to her. It had felt like a very long few weeks, almost a lifetime without her.

Joe had new friends, of course, but it wasn't the same depth of friendship. He could hardly remember his life before Violet, never sure which one of them had arrived in the children's block first. They were babies, or little toddlers, whichever they were, it was far too long ago for them to remember it. He knew it was the same for Violet; they had always had each other up until now.

Charlie, notwithstanding, Joe had only ever been able to discuss his mother with Violet. He might easily tell Charlie that his mother doesn't do so well, but he certainly wouldn't tell him that she was slowly but surely going *'round the bend'*. He'd told Violet that, and he'd told her without any fear. Violet would keep his confidence even if she had to keep it for the rest of her life, Joe knew that much.

He also knew that his mother was getting worse week by week. There was a very good reason for him having a face like a boy who had walked into a door, just as Charlie had declared. Joe could see that his mother's condition was worsening, and she not only talked about the long-dead grandmother that he'd never met, but she spoke as if she was still a married woman. A woman with a husband at home, not a widow trapped in the never-ending cycle of life in the workhouse. She was becoming a little manic with it, her pale blue eyes strangely bright with excitement as she talked of hurrying home at the end of the working day to be with her husband. She had even told Joe she was expecting her first baby, and it had almost stopped his heart. *Who did she think he was?* She'd only ever had one baby, and that baby was Joe. If, in her world, he had yet to be born, what was Joe to her now? Did she even love him like she used to? Worse still, how long would it be before she gave herself away to others? Would the Mistress or the Master overhear her and have her sent away to Cane Hill to be chained to a wall all day and all night?

Joe couldn't form a complete picture in his mind of the Cane Hill Asylum, all he could imagine was a stone-walled prison cell with heavy chains bolted to the wall, his mother's thin limbs held steady at the end of them. The bread almost turned to dust in his mouth, it was so dry. He needed to eat, but suddenly it was the last thing he wanted. In the end, Joe was forced to break off small pieces and swallow them down with little gulps of water.

Was there nothing to be enjoyed in life anymore, not even a lump of stale bread and a tin mug full of cold water?

Later in the evening, Joe found he couldn't get his mother out of his mind. She really had deteriorated so much in just one week that he began to wonder how much she had deteriorated in the few days since he had last seen her. An hour after the oil lamps had been extinguished, Joe was still wide awake. His mind was turning over and over, and he began to wonder if he could sneak through the moonlit corridors of the workhouse and find her. He just wanted to look at her, to see her sleeping peacefully so that he might do likewise.

Even knowing that it was a fool's errand, Joe had a stout soul, the sort of spirit that might keep him alive until he was a hundred years old. He got up out of bed and crept out of the dark boys' dormitory and into the corridor beyond. There was no sign of a warden out there now; he was probably taking a little swig of liquor somewhere in a quiet cupboard. Whatever he was doing, Joe was glad of it.

Being not entirely sure where the women's block was, Joe thought that he would, if he was quiet and stealthy, surely find it sooner or later. The high windows in the walls cast strange light in the corridors as the moonlight fell in patches. He hurried through the bright patches, taking his rest in the darkness that was spaced intermittently along the length of the corridor. He listened for any sound, ducking into deep doorways now and again in case somebody was coming his way.

When Joe reached a junction in the corridor, he stood for a moment, hoping that his eight-year-old's instinct would tell him which the right path was to take. In the end, realising that it didn't matter how long he stood there thinking about it, Joe turned left and hurried along in the darkness.

The corridor began to open out into a wider space with narrow alleyways disappearing this way and that. He could hear voices and froze for a moment before he realised that the voices were simply emanating from one of the narrow alleyways. He crept up to the edge of the corridor from which the voices came and leaned with his back flat against it for a few minutes. Silent, breathing as shallowly as he could, he listened intently, making sure that somebody wasn't about to come out and find him.

"And I'm being paid handsomely for it too!" The words were slurred, self-satisfied, and unmistakably those of the Master, Micah Turner.

"We have to make our money where we can, Mr Turner," the second voice, also male, could have been just about any one of the sycophantic cronies whom Joe always imagined lying face down in puddles so that Micah might walk across their backs and not get his feet wet.

"Don't we just! Don't we just!"

They seemed to be deep in conversation, Joe knew he ought to keep moving. Perhaps this would be his best chance to find his ma, and yet his curiosity had got the better of him. He remained with his back flat against the wall listening.

"And she doesn't know anything about it then?" the warden went on.

"She? Who?" Micah Turner's words were more slurred than Joe had realised, and it was clear that he had taken far too much strong liquor that night. He seemed not only drunk but also boastful.

"The girl," the warden went on. "Violet, what's her name… Marsh. She doesn't know anything about it?"

"Of course not!" the Master said and chuckled mercilessly. "The game would be up then, wouldn't it? No, the wretched creature has no idea who she is."

"So, you've been paid the whole time she's been here?"

"Nye-on six years now!" Micah laughed again, and Joe thought he sounded very, very pleased with himself.

Joe couldn't have moved away now if his life depended on it. They were talking about Violet, for there was no other Violet Marsh in the entire workhouse. He was sure of it. But who was she and why did she have no idea who she was? It didn't really make sense, and Joe wanted to know more.

"Oliver Daventry daren't not pay me now, dare he? I know too much, don't I? A scandal like that could ruin the man, couldn't it? No, a gentlemen like him don't want their secrets flying around London like tuberculosis, do they?"

"No more they do," the warden said, his sycophantic laughter aggravating Joe's very bones.

Joe hardly dared to breathe as he continued to listen to all that Micah Turner had to say in his drunken, boastful state. He heard it all and knew he would have to find a way to tell Violet. It was earth-shattering news, and Joe concentrated hard, wanting to commit the ins and outs of it all to memory. Finally, when Micah had spilled his guts entirely and talked himself dry, his mind turned to other things.

"Why don't you run down to the cellar and get us some more beer? Today's been my payday, you see, and I'm feeling generous," Micah snorted, and Joe suddenly panicked.

Without waiting to see what happened next, Joe turned on his heels and hastened back the way he'd come. His bare feet made a slight thumping noise on the cold flagstone floor, but he felt suddenly vulnerable in his new white nightshirt, the nightshirt which seemed almost to glow every time he hit a patch of moonlight in the corridor.

However, when he turned into the junction that he had lately turned out of, he breathed a sigh of relief; as far as he was concerned, Joe had escaped unseen.

The following morning, in the swell of people leaving the chapel, Violet realised that Joe had sneakily made his way to her side for the first time in weeks. It was a risky manoeuvre, but she was so pleased to see him that she could have cried.

"Keep your eyes front, Vi, act like I'm not talking to you," Joe was whispering, barely making a sound.

"Why? What's the matter?" she whispered back, careful to keep her eyes front just as he had told her to.

"Last night, I found out a secret. It's a big secret, even though I don't know all the details. But it's a secret about you, Violet, about who you are. Who you *really* are, I think," he said, and turned his head just a little. He was looking at her face, and she turned just enough that with her eyes as far right as to cause pain, she could just about see him.

"What secret? What do you mean who I really am?" she asked, and her heart began to pound. This felt important, so important that she was almost afraid to hear the rest.

"Gossiping, boy?" Suddenly, the Master himself was between them. He came at them from behind, his thick arm wrapping around Joe's neck and shoulders and drawing him sharply away. "Then, he was right. There was somebody!" Micah Turner went on, and Violet, terrified, had absolutely no idea what he was talking about.

Violet stood stock still and watched as Joe was pulled away from her. The Master was dragging him along until one of the wardens dashed up to help, and the two men each took an arm and carted him away. Instinctively, Violet knew that he was in dreadful trouble, and suddenly, her feet were moving again as she made to follow.

However, she was stopped in her tracks when somebody gripped a handful of the loose fabric of her shapeless shift dress and held her. She turned her head to find Vera Packham looming over her, her heavy jaw and long nose bearing down on her.

"Just where do you think you're going? Where do you think you're going to when you are about to be given a breakfast that you haven't yet earned?"

"Nowhere, Mistress," Violet said, knowing that there was no point in arguing; she had never had a voice in that place before, and she certainly didn't have one now. Nobody around her cared about Joe, not one of them. Not the wardens, not the other inmates. They were all too busy surviving from one end of the day to the other to care about the plight of another. Even if that other was just an eight-year-old boy, thin, vulnerable, brave, and kind-hearted.

All Violet could do now was concentrate on her work until their midday bread and water and hope that she would see Joe there too, unharmed in the dining hall.

Violet looked for Joe at every meal, but it had been almost a week since she had seen him in the swell of people leaving the chapel. At first, she had told herself that she hadn't looked properly, that her caution not to be caught had made her an ineffective searcher. In the end, however, she couldn't lie to herself any longer. Joe just wasn't there, and she had no idea where he was. Was he even still in the workhouse? Perhaps the Master had beaten him so badly that even now he languished in the infirmary, his little body battered and broken. Just the thought of it made her eyes swell with tears.

"What's the matter with you now, you workshy little brat?" Millie said sharply, and Violet looked down at her lap, where she had dropped the piece of rope she'd been working on. Without a word, Violet picked it up again and continued, not even turning her head to look at Millie. When was the horrible girl going to be moved away to the women's block? She was fifteen years old, and it was the time that she was no longer with the girls. Violet couldn't help but wonder if Vera Packham kept her there because she enjoyed the way Millie frightened the younger girls. It certainly wouldn't surprise her.

"You're still worried about your little friend, are you?" Millie went on and gave a snort of laughter. "You are, aren't you?"

Again, Violet said nothing. It occurred to her to wonder how it was Millie knew of her concerns, but a quick look in Jeanette's direction didn't leave her wondering for long. Despite her whispered apology, it seemed that Jeanette was the same tattle-tale she'd been before, and she had run to Millie with her latest piece of information and had parted with it in hopes of saving herself. Well, that would be the last time that Violet spoke to Jeanette about anything. She would never trust her again.

"If the Master himself dragged the boy away and he hasn't been seen since then, it's obvious what's happened, isn't it?" Millie was in a horrible, taunting mood, and Violet knew that she wasn't going to simply let it go, not even if Violet stayed silent.

"Is it?" Violet said coldly.

"He's dead. Of course, he's dead," Millie said, assuming an air of knowledge and wisdom and a little superiority; she was fifteen years old, after all.

"No, he's not dead. He isn't dead! Don't say such a horrible thing, Millie!" Before Violet had even finished her sentence, she felt a painful and resounding slap on the back of her neck. "Ouch!"

There then came the sound of heavy, clipping footsteps in the corridor outside, and all the girls immediately turned their attention to their rope. The Mistress was coming, and if she asked who was making so much noise, Violet had no doubt at all that each and every one of them would give *her* away and not *Millie*.

"What's all this? Who cried out?" Nobody said anything, but enough eyes flicked in Violet's direction that the Mistress soon honed in on her. "Violet Marsh, was that you?"

"Yes, Mistress. Sorry, Mistress."

"And why did you shout?"

"I'm sorry, Mistress, some of the oakum worked its way inside my finger again, and it took me by surprise," Violet answered neatly, even though she knew she had most certainly not shouted. For reasons of her own, Vera Packham had taken a firm dislike to Violet, and Violet knew it would do her no good to protest too much.

"Well, get back to your work and stay silent. If I hear another peep out of you, I will send you to the Master, and *he* will deal with you." It was a threat, pure and simple.

Even though the girls in the workhouse were not to be physically punished as the boys were, it was hardly a secret that they were. Fortunately, Vera Packham didn't seem to go in for such things herself, beyond a verbal berating and the occasional gripping of the girls' clothes, a little pushing, and shoving, perhaps. But the girls *were* punished, now and again. Perhaps even the women were too, but Violet hadn't heard anything about that.

Micah Turner was not a man who followed the regulations, not unless it suited his purposes to do so. For the Mistress to say she would send her to that man was enough to fill Violet's heart with genuine dread.

"Yes, Mistress," Violet said, nodding and hardly daring to look up in Vera's direction.

Within minutes of the Mistress wandering away to check that the wardens in the women's block were doing their work properly, Millie started up again.

"He's dead, and that lunatic mother of his is finally where she is meant to be!" Millie turned in her seat, and Violet could feel her rotten little eyes on her. "Don't you want to know where?"

"No," Violet said; if it was true, then she already knew where.

"She's been carted away to the Cane Hill Asylum with the rest of the nutters, hasn't she?" Millie said, and a little titter of frightened amusement broke out amongst the other girls. "She's chained to a wall rocking and drooling and talking nonsense, and she'll be there until the day she dies. Maybe it would be better if she died right away, for the Cane Hill Asylum is a much crueller place than the workhouse could ever be." Millie was enjoying herself, and Violet couldn't help but hate her for it.

"You've got the ugliest, blackest heart of anybody I ever met, Millie. One day the worms that live in your chest will eat away at you until there's nothing left. Every ugly thing you say will come back at you, it will taunt you, and you'll suffer for it." Violet turned to glare viciously at the older girl and was pleased when Millie's eyes widened with surprise. Even Violet was surprised at herself. She had never said anything aggressive or cruel before in her life.

"What if I hit you again? Yes, what if I hit you again and you cry out? You'll be sent to Micah Turner then. Yes, I think that would be a very fitting punishment for the way you just spoke to me." And with that, Millie slapped her hard on the back of the neck again.

This time, however, Violet uttered not one sound. She gritted her teeth, determined that she would take whatever Millie threw at her, and never once cried out. Millie hit her again, harder this time, but Violet, despite the pain, simply continued to pick at the piece of rope. When Millie hit her once again, Violet felt a rush of determination race through her body. She felt suddenly as if she had a little control over her life, even if it was just control over her own reactions. Whatever it was, it was better than nothing. Whatever it was, it made her suddenly feel a little powerful.

Millie leaned forward and peered into her face, hoping to see tears rolling down her cheeks, no doubt. However, dry-eyed, eight-year-old Violet simply smiled at her.

"Keep beating me if you like, Millie, I won't make a sound. But when the Mistress asks me why I am black and blue, when she wants to know who did it, I will tell her. I swear to you, I will. So, yes, Millie, you just keep beating me if you like."

There was a sharp intake of breath from all around her, every one of the frightened girls even more frightened as they wondered what would happen next. Or perhaps it was admiration; after all, none of them had stood up to Millie themselves, had they? None of them had stood up to the girl who was almost a woman, apart from the child who was only just eight years old.

When Millie turned back to her own work, Violet knew that she had won, for now, at least. But what had she won? She thought of Joe and his mother, of the poor woman now chained to a wall and suffering as her own mind crumbled. And what of Joe? Was he really dead? Had Micah Turner really killed him? Her heart was broken, but just like the vicious slaps that Millie had dished out, Violet Marsh would never make a sound again.

CHAPTER 5

By the time Violet Marsh reached fourteen years of age, the hateful Millie was just a distant memory. She saw her from time to time, of course, although she'd never particularly looked out for her in the dining hall or the chapel. Millie had been moved into the women's block five and a half years before, and there had been nobody of a similar nature to replace her, thankfully.

The girls weren't particularly close, not like Violet and Joe had been. They didn't open their hearts to one another, nor did Violet want them to. All she had was control over herself outwardly, even if she did not always have it inwardly.

"I wonder what it will be like with the women," Jeanette said quietly one day as the group of girls, smaller than it had been for a while, worked diligently at their oakum picking.

"I'm sure you will be just fine, Jeanette," Violet said, not wanting to frighten Jeanette about her own near future, even though she had never forgotten her crimes of six years before when Violet had first joined the girls' block. "I've never heard anything bad about the women's block."

"I don't know so much, have you seen Millie these days?" Jeanette asked fearfully.

"Yes, but perhaps it has nothing to do with the other women." Violet kept her eyes on her ropework and chewed thoughtfully at her bottom lip.

She had seen Millie and had noticed how she looked worse and worse as each day passed. But it was a new thing, for surely, she had only started to deteriorate in appearance these last months. Could that really be attributed to the other women she worked with? Surely, it couldn't even be attributed to Vera Packham. But there was something wrong with her, there was no doubt about it.

Millie, who had once seemed *almost* pretty, now looked ten years older than her true age, painfully thin, with a white face and dark rings around her eyes. Violet had studied her from time to time, and couldn't help but feel pity for her even after how cruel and hateful Millie had been. No one deserved whatever she was going through, no matter how vindictive they were. However, there was more to it than simply how she looked. Violet had seen how she often turned suddenly to look over her shoulder as if she expected to see some fearful sight directly behind her. When she wasn't looking over her shoulder, she twitched involuntarily and often picked at her clothes and even her hair. Where she once had thick hair, she seemed to have picked it away until it was nothing but thin, dry strands. She looked as if she had some dreadful illness, and Violet began to wonder if that might be the truth of it.

"My fingers hurt," Mary, just eight years old and only in the girls' block the last two weeks, spoke in a choked little voice. Violet looked over and could see that the little girl was crying.

"Jeanette, keep an eye out, would you?" Violet said, and Jeanette hurried to the open door, peering around the frame and along the corridor. She turned back to Violet and nodded; the coast was clear.

Violet put her rope down on top of the pile of oakum in her own basket and crossed the room to where little Mary was sitting. She sat down next to her and put her arm around her shoulders, pulling the little girl into her and comforting her.

"Let me see," Violet said and took Mary's rope from her tiny hands so that she might inspect her fingers. The fingers were red raw, some of them bleeding, and she could see how the tiny fibres had made their way into the soft skin.

"It hurts, I can't keep picking this dreadful stuff," Mary was beginning to sound panic-stricken, and Violet knew she would have to do everything in her power to keep calm.

"Keep the rope in your hands, but stop picking. I will put some of my oakum in your basket, and that will keep the Mistress from chastising you. You can let your hands rest today, but you'll have to try again tomorrow. You have to let the skin harden, you see, for that's the only way to get used to it. Once your skin is hard, the little fibres can't get in, do you see?" Violet pulled the little girl against her once again and wrapped her arms around her, holding her tightly. "It will be all right, Mary, it will be all right."

"Thank you, Violet," Mary said and choked back a sob.

"Whatever you're going to do, you'd better get on with it. Fearsome Vera is on her way back!" Jeanette hissed and raced across the room to retake her seat. She grinned when there was a titter of laughter at the amusing name that she'd given the Mistress. Perhaps Violet would miss her just a little when she went.

"Here you go," Violet said in a whisper as she put two handfuls of freshly picked oakum into Mary's basket. She was heartened to see three other girls putting a handful in too, showing a little solidarity to the new and frightened eight-year-old girl.

Violet was clever, calm, and thought by some to be fearless. She wasn't really fearless, but the older ones had seen how she had taken on Millie when she was just a child, and how she had taken her on without flinching. She knew she was popular among the other girls, but she never allowed herself to grow close to any of them. Even after six years, she still mourned the loss of her dear childhood friend, and she was determined never, ever to feel that loss again.

When Vera Packham strode into the room, there was not a sound to be heard. All the girls concentrated hard on their rope, and Vera walked up and down the room, peering into the baskets.

"You seem to be doing well there, Mary," Vera said, being so surprised to see so much oakum in the little girl's basket that she forgot herself and gave ready praise. With her head down, Violet secretly smiled to herself.

"You could do to get on with it, Marsh!" Vera said sharply, still calling Violet by her second name as she had done for six years now.

"Yes, Mistress," Violet said, carrying on with her work without looking up.

"I don't want you thinking you can slacken off, because you can't. I expect you to work as hard as everybody else. Look here, girl, there's a child here who seems to have worked twice as hard as you have today. You should be ashamed of yourself. You may not flutter your eyelashes at me and think that it will get you anywhere."

"Of course, Mistress," Violet said, seething so badly that she couldn't help herself but continued. "But then I do not flutter my eyelashes at anybody."

"And just who do you think you're talking to? You still rely on the charity of the workhouse just as you have done all your life and yet you think you are somebody, don't you? Let me tell you, Violet Marsh, that you are *not* somebody; you are *nobody*. You came here alone; you will die here alone. You are still no better than the abandoned child you began your life as. Get on with it!" Vera Packham seemed rattled and marched out of the room.

Violet finally raised her head and stared after the vile woman as she marched away. It wasn't the first time that she had made some illusion to Violet's appearance, most particularly her eyelashes, and Violet knew exactly what the problem was.

She was not yet fifteen, but Violet was fast becoming a beautiful young woman. She had thick glossy brown hair, which she kept determinedly clean. When she pinned it up out of the way, it held its shape nicely and always shone, despite the deficiencies in the workhouse meals. She had clear skin and large brown eyes; she had seen herself in the one and only mirror that the girls were permitted to use to make sure that their hair was neat and tidy.

Nonetheless, Violet was not a vain girl. She truly didn't care if she was beautiful or not, she just wanted to survive the workhouse, to find some way out of it. To somebody like Vera Packham, a woman who seemed to become more masculine by the day, Violet's beauty was beginning to seem like an insult. Just by existing, Violet was a reminder of everything that Vera was not, and Vera Packham didn't like that one little bit.

When the Mistress returned to the room so quickly, Violet was not the only girl to be surprised. She looked every bit as angry as she had looked on her way out of the room, and Violet had the dreadful sense that something was coming. Vera had one of the wardens in tow, and she looked at him earnestly before pointing her finger almost right into Violet's face.

"That one! Yes, that's the one! You will need to take her to the delousing room."

"Delousing room?" Violet said and threw her rope down into her basket and rose to her feet. "I do not need to go to the delousing room, I do not have lice."

"How dare you argue with me, girl? If I look in your hair and I see lice, then something will be done about it, do you understand me? I will not have you infecting every girl in the hall. Never mind every girl in the hall, everybody in the chapel or the dining hall. If I'm lenient with you, the entire workhouse will be lousy. No, get a hold of her. Drag her if you have to." The Mistress was breathing hard, and her wide nostrils flared.

As the warden approached her, Violet stepped over the low bench and began to back away. However, she backed herself into the corner of the room and stood there helplessly as the man moved closer, something of an uncertain look in his eyes.

"Sir, I do not have lice," Violet said, her voice beseeching, her eyes pleading with his. At that moment, she knew that he was entirely aware that she didn't have lice, but he looked so apologetic that she also knew that he was going to do the Mistress' bidding no matter what. If he didn't, he would likely have Micah Turner to answer to, and perhaps he was almost as afraid as one of the inmates might have been.

With a painfully kind look, he took her arm. Violet snatched her arm away from him, but he just took her arm again, this time more firmly.

"Don't make this more difficult, girl. Don't make this harder than it has to be." His voice was quiet and as apologetic as his expression had been. Violet wanted to scratch his eyes out, to call him the very coward that he was. She was reminded of the warden who had stood awkwardly that day as Micah Turner had almost beaten the skin clean off Joe Willis. In some ways, they were worse, the men who felt sorry for them and yet did nothing. Not quite Micah Turner's sycophants, but certainly afraid of him, too afraid of him to do the right thing.

Even though the warden was so much bigger than she, Violet struggled valiantly. In the end, Vera Packham herself darted across the room and seized her flailing arm, dragging her out into the corridor beyond with the help of the warden.

Violet kicked wildly and tried to free herself all the way along the corridor to the delousing room. It was a room that was commonly used to remove the lice from the clothes of the people who had just lately been accepted into the workhouse. The clothing was steamed until the lice were killed, and it was stored so that the new inmates might collect that clothing if they ever decided to leave the workhouse.

Despite the deprivations of the workhouse, head lice did not often have the chance to travel widely. New inmates were so thoroughly and inhumanely scoured for such things that they were scrupulously clean when they first made their way to one of the dormitories. The very notion that Violet had lice was ridiculous, and she beseeched the warden all the way to the delousing room to take one look at her scalp, for he would declare her to be clean.

However, the warden ignored her pleas, hardening himself to her and saying nothing more to her throughout the rest of the appalling experience. He helped Vera drag her into the delousing room. The door shut behind them as he held her down onto a chair, his arms pinning hers to her sides whilst Vera took the scissors to her.

Vera dragged out the pins that Violet had so carefully slid into her head just that morning, letting them fall to the flagstone floor, making a curious tinkling sound as they did. As Violet tried to twist her head away, Vera wound a thick tendril of hair around her fist and pulled it up sharply. The pain in her scalp was so great that Violet was forced to stop struggling. In no time at all, the Mistress had cut Violet's hair as short as a man's hair. When it was done, Violet simply went limp, tears rolling down her face as she stared down at the thick waves of shiny brown hair lying in little piles on the floor all around her.

When she saw Vera Packham looking at just the same, she saw a little smile of triumph on the evil woman's face. Finally, it seemed that Vera had got what she wanted; she had made Violet Marsh ugly. She had dehumanised her, humiliated her, and in so doing, she had elevated herself.

"Stop, girl, stop right there."

Violet, who had been ferrying the full baskets of oakum to the storeroom, stood stock still. She had been halted by none other than the Master himself, and Micah Turner was not a man to be ignored.

Violet said nothing, she simply stood there holding onto the basket, her eyes turned down in what she hoped was a respectful way.

"What happened?" he said and took a step closer to her. He was such a big man that his presence, even though he was still easily a foot away from her, could be felt almost like a physical touch. "Why does your hair look like that? Why have you cut it?" He seemed vexed by her sudden change in appearance.

Even though Violet still wore the little poke hat over her shorn hair, the fact that it was so short was still quite clearly apparent.

"The Mistress cut it, Master," Violet said, her mouth dry and her palms perspiring. She couldn't have any interaction with Micah Turner and not think about Joe Willis. Had he really killed him all those years ago? When she had seen him beat Joe that day, she had intervened herself because she was certain that he wouldn't stop until Joe was dead. She knew him to be capable of killing, she just knew it.

"The Mistress cut your hair? And why did she do that, Violet?" He seemed annoyed, but Violet rather thought that he was more annoyed with Vera Packham than her.

"The Mistress declared that I had lice, Master," Violet said, her generous lips suddenly set in a thin line as she thought of the dreadful pain and humiliation of that day.

"And did you?"

"It is not for me to go against the Mistress, Master," Violet said, knowing that to be anything but politic in this situation would risk her very safety. She could trust neither the Mistress nor the Master and could hardly say which of them would turn on her first.

"Well, you are to tell her that she will not do that again." His words were so surprising that Violet's mouth fell open. "No, don't do that. I will tell her; you need not think about it."

"Thank you, Master," Violet said, despising him down to his very bone marrow but knowing that she could do no other than show at least a little gratitude for what appeared to be his genuine concern.

"Although no woman looks fair of face when her hair is cut so horribly short, I must say that you are rather surprising. Yes, quite surprising indeed," he said and took another step towards her. He was so tall that he had to lean forward, stooping a little so that he might study her face at close quarters. "Yes, I must declare that you still have a pretty face. Yes, it is a credit to you that you still have a pretty look about you even though your hair is cut so close to your head. Perhaps you are a natural. Yes, perhaps that is it," he went on, his voice rather vague, and his eyes seeming a little glazed. It was almost as if he had no idea that he was speaking the words aloud, but rather letting them roll silently through his mind.

He didn't speak for some moments, but he didn't move away, either. Gripping the handles of the basket, Violet's hands began to perspire more and more, and she silently prayed that the basket wouldn't slip from her grasp. The more he stared at her, the more uncomfortable she became. His face was so close to hers that she could smell a little foulness on his breath, although perhaps not as foul as some others she had encountered in her time at the workhouse. She thought that the foulness was perhaps on account of strong liquor, although her experience of such things was so minute that she couldn't be at all sure that she was right. Whatever the smell was, she didn't like it one little bit.

"Why do you not look at me, girl?" he said, but his tone wasn't an angry one. There was an amused edge to it, almost as if he was teasing her in a friendly way. It was so unsettling that her heart began to pound, and she felt more uncomfortable still. "Why are your eyes down? Raise them up; look at me."

It took an effort of will for Violet to roll her eyes upward and look at his face. She couldn't look into his eyes, she had long feared those dreadful, coal-black orbs full of evil. Instead, she fixed upon his nose, marking its broadness, its thousands of tiny dot-like pores, it's broken veins.

"There now, that wasn't so difficult, was it?" Once again, she was assaulted by his foul breath.

"No, Master," she said, her mouth so dry now that her tongue almost stuck to its roof.

Suddenly, there was the sound of footsteps somewhere distant along the corridor, and Violet was grateful for it, for the noise seemed to bring Micah Turner back to his senses. He straightened up and took a step back from her, giving her a final look before releasing her.

"Well, you'd better get to wherever it is you're going, girl. Go on, quick smart!" he said, and he was so fully returned to himself that it was almost as if the last few moments had never happened.

"No, he's never come up to me like that before. I mean, with that kind of look. You'd better watch out, Violet." Jeanette's eyes were wide with mawkish interest.

"I don't know exactly, but, well, I…"

"You know. That's the thing, isn't it? We all know, us girls, when a man is being familiar in that kind of way. The wardens do it, some of them, you must know that."

"Yes, they do," Violet said fearfully. "But they don't dare do anything about it. With a man like Micah Turner, he has nobody there to tell him he can't." Once again, she remembered how the warden had stood by as the Master almost killed Joe. "I might just be making things worse in my head."

"That's just wishful thinking, Vi. He's done it before," Jeanette said, enjoying leaving the tantalising comment in mid-air.

"What do you mean?"

"There was talk of a girl who'd just moved up into the women's block. Annie, her name was. Anyway, she'd managed to get hold of some liquor. I don't know, I suppose she went out of the grounds and got it for herself. When she was caught, Fearsome Vera dragged her to the Master. You know how she gets." Jeanette raised her eyebrows.

"Yes, I do," Violet said, and subconsciously ran her hand through her cropped hair.

"Well, the girl came out of his office and said he'd punished her. He'd made her lean over his desk, and he beat her behind. Only he didn't hurt her."

"Perhaps because he isn't supposed to punish the female inmates."

"Not according to the girl. She said he spent a good amount of time with her, and he wasn't so much beating her as..." Jeanette trailed off. "They say she wasn't too concerned about it; she was just glad to get away unbruised."

"*They* say? You mean you don't know this for certain?"

"It was a few years ago now. I'd only just moved into the girls' block as this Annie woman was moved out. Millie found out most of the details. You know what she was like."

"I do!" Violet said, already determined to treat the whole thing as fiction; it certainly made her feel better to do so.

"But it's not made up, Vi. The girl, Annie, well, Micah, kept on sending for her. It was supposed to be to check on her drinking, but everybody knew what was going on. He just kept doing the same thing to her. Then, after a while, he moved on to other things."

"What other things?"

"Come on, Vi! You know what I mean!"

"And that's what this Annie is supposed to have said, is it?"

"She told bits and pieces to people, but it was her health which was most telling. She began to get thin, and she looked afraid all the time. Whatever he was doing to her, it was a lot worse than a bit of touching, mark my words."

"So, what happened? Is she still here?"

"No, she's not. She began to go *'round the bend* a bit, and everyone thought she'd soon be carted off to Cane Hill." Jeanette pointed at her own head to indicate mental illness. "But before they had a chance to take her away, she ran away. Or at least, that was the story we were told. Everyone was terrified when it happened, so nobody asked too many questions."

Violet felt suddenly sick; she had a vague recollection of hearing the tale of the woman who had disappeared. Joe had told her about it. It was the element of truth to the story of Annie, which made the rest of it now seem so much more plausible than it had been just moments before.

"That's awful." Her voice hardly sounded like her own. "They can just do what they like to us in here, can't they? It's like we're not real people at all." Tears started to roll down her face.

"You just make sure you keep out of his way, Vi. Just hope he sets his sights on somebody else."

Somebody else? How could she wish that on somebody else? At that moment, she thought of Millie. The once bold and cocky girl who seemed to have become a haunted, frightened young woman. Was Micah Turner the cause?

CHAPTER 6

For the next few months, Violet did manage to keep away from the Master. She saw him, of course, but they had never crossed each other's path in so isolated a way as they had done on the day that he'd made her so uncomfortable.

Violet was so determined not to get into trouble of any kind, which might see the rotten Vera Packham send her to him that she hardly spoke a word. She worked hard, she kept her head down, and she tried to stay beneath Vera's notice.

Jeanette, being now fifteen, had been sent to the women's block, and Violet, at fourteen, was now the oldest girl in the group. She was still kind to the little ones, but her greatest kindness was encouraging them to be kind to one another. She didn't want to feel responsible for them, lest she found herself defending them in a way that might throw her onto Micah Turner's path.

For a while, things seemed to go along without incident. That was until Vera Packham called her out of the workroom where Violet was sitting on her bench oakum picking.

"Marsh!" she said in her usual, aggravated tone of voice. She said no more, just beckoned her out of the room with a crooked finger.

Violet followed her out of the room and down the corridor until they reached the tiny room that the Mistress used as her own office.

"You are to be moved, Marsh." Vera stood in the middle of the little room with her hands on her hips. Violet stood by the closed door, not sure if she was expected to advance any further into the room.

"To the women's block?" Violet asked sheepishly; she was too young, surely.

"No, you are to still sleep in the girls' block, but you won't be oakum picking. No, you've been moved to help with food preparation. A plum job!" she added the last with venom.

"Yes, Mistress," Violet said, not daring to argue.

"Seems to me that you lead something of a charmed life here, Marsh!" Vera went on waspishly. "One minute, I'm not allowed to cut your lousy hair, the next, you are given an easy job. I have to wonder what it is you do to receive such special consideration. What little services you provide when my back is turned."

"Services?" Violet asked, but she was already beginning to understand the insinuation. "Mistress, I do no such thing. I work, I eat, and I sleep. You may ask any of the other girls. Indeed, the warden who watches over the girls' dormitory at night. You may ask anybody!" Her voice was rising in anger.

"Don't take that tone with me. You might be a favourite with the Master, but you are still under my control."

"I would hope never to be anybody's favourite in this Godforsaken place!" Violet was still angry. Vera slapped her hard across the face, but Violet simply recovered herself immediately and glared at her defiantly, holding the woman's gaze so unflinchingly that Vera was the first to look away.

"Well, I shall take you to the kitchens so that you may be told your new duties," the Mistress went on as if the previous few minutes had never happened. "Come, let's not dawdle!"

As Violet cut lettuce and picked tomatoes from the large vegetable plot at the back of the workhouse, the weak sunshine on her back made her feel human. It wasn't warm enough that a person could sit out on a bench in a fine London park, but it was certainly warm enough for a young woman working hard.

Her hair had grown back and was now long enough that it needed to be tied away from her face in a small bun at the back of her head. Something about that made her feel human, and it gave her the very smallest victory over the appalling Vera Packham.

She still came into great contact with the Mistress, but perhaps not as much as when she had been oakum picking with the other girls. The rest of the women who worked with her now, the ones who undertook any necessary domestic task to keep the workhouse running, were all older than Violet. The youngest of them were in their twenties and the oldest, perhaps in their fifties.

There had been none of the bullying that she'd experienced when she'd moved from the children's block to the girls' block. Violet had braced herself, fully expecting it, but it hadn't come. She realised that females like Millie in the workhouse were the exception rather than the rule, and she drew some comfort from it.

"How many have we got, Violet?" Jane, one of the younger women at perhaps twenty-three, asked.

"Ten lettuces ready to be eaten and two baskets of tomatoes. Will that be enough? There are some nearly ripe tomatoes, but I think they might be better picked tomorrow."

"That's more than enough," Jane said, lifting her striped dress just a little as she plodded her way across the vegetable patch. "Here, let me take one of the tomato baskets."

"Thank you," Violet said, smiling. She liked Jane, who was a sensible woman. She was bright and simply got on with her day without poking her nose into anybody else's business or making miserable comments. There was something about the young woman, which made Violet sometimes forget that she was in the workhouse. It was almost as if the two of them worked in service together somewhere, far away from this awful place, earning a real living.

Violet and Jane got along well without really knowing very much about each other. Violet was glad of it; she didn't want to get too close to her. It was nice to work with somebody who made things seem normal, and there were very few inmates at the workhouse who could do that much for her.

Of course, gossip being what it is, one of the other women had already informed Violet that Jane had been forced to come to the workhouse as a young woman who was *with* child and *without* a husband. In no time at all, the infant was removed from Jane's care. The guardians decided that Jane was a moral degenerate who couldn't possibly raise the child well, inside or outside of the workhouse. It made Violet angry in a way that made her belly burn when she thought about it. Just because some feckless young man hadn't bothered to take responsibility for his own child didn't mean that Jane wasn't prepared to. They all judged in this awful place, but they only judged the poor. They never judged those who abused their power, their authority, those who meted out violence and cruelty day in day out. When would they be judged?

"We've got a lovely job this afternoon, you and me!" Jane said conversationally as the two women walked along.

"Oh, yes?"

"We're scrubbing the corridor floors from one end of the workhouse to the other." Jane laughed.

"I'm looking forward to it already," Violet said and laughed. That was the best thing about being outside gathering up vegetables, there was very rarely somebody there to oversee you. It was a place where a person could really laugh and not have scorn poured on them for it. It was a little slice of freedom.

All in all, Violet was enjoying her new work. And after four months of it, she felt so secure that she no longer bothered to question who had decided to move her and why.

On the day that question came into her mind again, Violet was so surprised she felt angry with herself. Why hadn't she seen this coming? Why hadn't she done something to guard against it? However, in the end, what could she have done, even if she had known? Nothing, that's what.

"Violet, you're to take this tray along to the Master's office," one of the two old ladies who generally spent their days cooking nodded her head at the tray set out on the large wooden food preparation table.

"To the Master's office?" Violet asked, suddenly panic-stricken. The panic only grew worse when she saw a look pass between the other women, a look of pity, a look of knowing. Whatever this was, did they know? Had they already suffered it themselves? Violet couldn't help but think of Millie, that once brash and confident young woman who was now riddled with involuntary ticks, thinning hair, and a haunted look.

"That's right!" Violet turned sharply to see Vera Packham standing in the corner of the kitchen, her arms folded tightly across her chest. "And look smart about it, Marsh! That soup will be cold if you don't hurry, and the Master won't be at all pleased about that. Come on!" she said and clapped her hands together twice to chivvy Violet along.

With trembling hands, Violet picked up the tray. It had been ten months now since that awful encounter in the corridor with Micah Turner, and she realised that she had lulled herself into a false sense of security, even turning the incident into nothing more than a misunderstanding on her part. Oh, how the mind works to protect one.

By the time she reached the door of the Master's office, Violet's throat was dry and raw. Awkwardly holding the tray, she knocked at the door.

"Come!" came the unmistakable voice from within. Trying to balance the tray and open the door at the same time caused a little of the soup to swim up to the brim of the bowl and make its way over the top. It wasn't much, but it was enough to make her nervous.

Violet entered the room without a word, advancing slowly, looking around for somewhere to put the tray. Micah Turner was sitting behind his desk, a great pile of papers disarranged all over the place. There wasn't a spare spot anywhere to put the tray down.

"Where should I put the tray, Master?"

"Just put it down in front of me," he said and indicated that she should simply set the tray on top of the paperwork. Either the paperwork wasn't important, or Micah Turner couldn't have cared less about it. Still, he'd told her to put the tray there, and so she did.

"The tray is a bit of a mess, isn't it?" he said, his black eyes surveying the soup, no more than a spoonful, which had splashed onto the tray.

"I'm sorry, Master," Violet said and wished she had a cloth

in the pocket of her apron to tidy it up with, but she didn't.

"Well, let's just see, shall we?" he said, lifting the spoon and thrusting it into the bowl. Violet wanted to get out of the room, but he hadn't given her leave to, and she didn't want to risk his wrath. When his blank look turned into one of extreme displeasure, and he dropped the spoon into the bowl, causing yet more of the liquid to fly out over the edge, Violet's heart began to pound. "Is there a reason why I am served cold soup, Violet?"

"No, Master. I came as quickly as I could. I'm very sorry," she said, feeling suddenly hot and sick.

"Firstly, there is soup all over the tray, and then the remainder in the bowl is cold. I do not believe for a minute that you came as quickly as you could, and I am not at all pleased by your lying to me." There was something in his expression, a flicker of pleasure, perhaps? Anticipation? Whatever it was, Violet realised that she had been set up entirely.

Whether the soup had been hot or cold, Micah Turner had already decided to use that as a prop in what she could now see was his little theatrical piece. And if she hadn't managed to slop a little of the soup onto the tray, he would undoubtedly have found some other reason to criticise her.

"I could forgive the state of the meal you have brought to me, child, but it is the lying which I cannot overlook.

You've lived here in the workhouse for most of your life, and I'm sure you realise that the larger part of our training for you and those like you is designed to urge you in the direction of leading a better life. I'm afraid the lying does not convince me that you have taken the training to your heart. I am bound to say that I'm very disappointed, not only for myself but for you. Not only have you let me down, you've let yourself down too. There can be no other solution to this little quandary but to punish you and live in the hope that you will think about this punishment and choose to do things differently in the future."

"Punishment?" Violet said, having the awful feeling that she already knew what was coming.

"That's right, punishment. Only physical punishment can keep you on the right path; the path to a good life."

"But, Master, the regulations," Violet said, starting to back away. "Girls are not supposed to be physically punished. It is against the regulations."

"And just who, exactly, are you going to tell? It's very clever of you to know, of course, but perhaps not so clever of you to say it out loud. There is nobody in this building above me, is there? Just who are you going to complain to, when all such complaints end up on my desk?" He was out from behind his desk now and moving towards her. Just as she reached the door, the Master did too, and he pushed it shut with a bang.

"Please, let me out."

"No," he said deadly serious. He took a step towards Violet, and smiled cruelly as he took in a theatrical breath – breathing in her scent. "I don't think I want you to leave just yet."

"Please, please, stop!" Violet said, and moved away from him. It was also away from the door, the only chance at escape, but she couldn't bear be to be close to the man. He was equal parts terrifying and revolting.

"How dare you? How dare you move away from me? How dare you think that you are good enough to reject me, Violet Marsh!" He looked angry now, and Violet was more and more afraid. "I was hoping we could be gentle with each other, but clearly not."

He raised a hand, enclosed in a fist and Violet cried out, just as there came a knock at the door, and a hapless warden strode in.

"Forgive me, Master," the warden said, reddening as he realised his mistake and standing awkwardly in the doorway. Violet took her opportunity to escape him and hurried out the door.

By the time she returned to the kitchen, she was already crying, her hair still loose, her hands shaking. Some of the women looked at her, pitying her, not knowing what to say. They knew what had happened, she was sure they did, but what could they do to help her? Nothing.

CHAPTER 7

"Are you absolutely sure about this, Violet?" Jane whispered to her as the two of them went about their afternoon cleaning duties.

"I can't stay here to be beaten and who knows what else, Jane. I would rather die than that, and if I die out on the streets, then so be it. But you're absolutely sure I can't just leave?"

"*I* can leave, any of the adults may leave, but *you* are a ward of the guardians. They may keep you here for as long as they see fit and claim it to be for your own good. They only have to claim something to be for the good of the child to have their own way, believe me." Jane's eyes told their own story; she was thinking of her own beloved infant.

"Then, I will have to run. I will have to sneak out in the dead of night."

"Then I suggest you come to the kitchen, Violet. Creep carefully through here in the darkness. I will make sure that the kitchen door is left unlocked. That way, you can go out through the vegetable plot, around the edge of the grounds, and then out through the old door in the high wall at the back. Do you know the one I mean? It is the door that is half covered in ivy. It's supposed to be locked, but it's so old and rotten, one good push would open it."

"Thank you, Jane. I don't know how I would manage this day without you."

"I wish you wouldn't go," Jane said and shook her head sadly. "You've never known anything but this place. To be out there on your own on the streets of London, I can hardly bear to think about it."

"Nothing out there can be worse than what I will endure if I stay here. I may have escaped the Master today, but I won't escape him tomorrow. He is determined, and he's furious that I rejected him. No, he won't leave this, he won't let it go. I have to escape, there's no other way."

"Of all people, I will miss you. But I understand, and I wish you all the luck in the world." Jane looked up and down the corridor until she was certain that there was nobody around before she pulled Violet into her arms and embraced her tightly. "Good luck, my sweet."

It was easy enough to escape from the workhouse, far easier than Violet would have imagined. She had no possessions but the awful striped dress that she was wearing, and the nightgown which she had carefully folded and tucked down the front of her dress. With her rough woollen shawl wrapped about her shoulders, Violet couldn't think about whether it would be enough to keep her warm once she was outside in the cold night air. All she could do was think of Micah Turner and let her fear of him motivate her, propel her forward.

When she had almost reached the kitchen, she encountered somebody there. She was so frightened that she'd almost cried out until she realised that the woman standing in front of her barely registered her presence. In the pale moonlight which fell across the corridors from the high windows, she could see that it was Millie. Without a word, she took Millie's elbow and gently led her into the kitchen, out of harm's way.

"Millie, what are you doing? Why aren't you in bed?" Violet asked gently, realising now that she felt more pity for Millie than she had ever felt hatred. She knew, without a doubt, that Millie had been suffering the very abuse that Violet was seeking to escape. That was what was wrong with her.

"Sometimes I like to hide," Millie said, and then grinned like a child. "Hide and seek. If I play hide and seek and I get really good at it, he might not be able to find me. Maybe he'll never find me again, and I'll be safe," she went on, growing more and more excited as her curious idea began to take hold of her.

"Do you mean the Master? Do you mean Micah Turner?" Violet asked gently.

Millie's eyes flew open wide, and she looked over her shoulder.

"Is he here? Oh, dear God, is he here?"

"No, Millie, he's not here. He is not here. Oh, poor Millie, come with me."

"But where?"

"I'm running away, Millie. I'm escaping this awful place. Come with me, just come with me, for goodness sake."

"I can't," Millie said and was momentarily returned to the same young woman she had once been. "This is what my life is meant to be, Violet. I will die in the workhouse. I pray it is sooner rather than later."

"Nobody's life is meant to be like this, Millie. Please, for your own sake, come with me."

"There is just one of him in here, but the world outside these walls is a terrifying place. There are Micah Turner's everywhere you look, all of them wanting to take what isn't theirs to take. But how do we stop them? How do we ever stop them?" Millie began to blink rapidly, and then she grinned at Violet again. Violet realised that the moment of lucidity had passed, as she knew that Millie wouldn't come with her.

Violet had to go, however. She couldn't wait and try to cajole Millie into leaving, there wasn't time. Millie was too afraid to go outside; Micah Turner had certainly seen to that. But if Violet didn't move now, she realised that she was simply, in looking at Millie, looking at her own future. And so, she kissed Millie tenderly on the cheek, put her finger to her lips, and darted out through the unlocked kitchen door.

Violet hadn't been out in the streets more than an hour before she realised that poor Millie would never have coped. It was dark, it was frightening, and there were all sorts of noises. Creeping footsteps in alleyways, little cries now and again from voices she could hardly discern as male or female, and the ever-present scuttling of rats.

Violet walked a little while until she could see the shining black water of the River Thames ahead of her. She made her way along a narrow street towards it, hardly knowing why, and was surprised to suddenly find herself staring up at the most beautiful cathedral. It seemed such a strange place for a cathedral, with everything around it being so dark and so grubby. Something about its sudden presence made her feel safe, and Violet crept through the darkness, trying to find the door.

Once she did, she was pleased to find it open and silently let herself in. There was a wooden plaque in the moonlit entrance reminding parishioners of the days and times of various services. Violet stopped to read it and realised that she was in Southwark Cathedral. She'd heard of it no end of times, different people who came and went from the workhouse often mentioned it. She'd known it was nearby but had never imagined that she would one day see it.

Creeping further into the cathedral, Violet was relieved that there were candles lit here and there and that the place wasn't in complete darkness. She looked up at the beautiful statues carved high above her, the extraordinary arched windows, the magnificent wooden ceiling. It was certainly a far cry from the chapel at the workhouse, and she gave a silent prayer of thanks for having stumbled upon it so quickly.

Still moving silently, she made her way down the aisle and into one of the pews. She sat down, leaning her back against the hard wood and wondering if she could sleep sitting up. Though she was exhausted, her nerves still jangled from her daring escape. Even so, in no time at all, her eyelids felt heavy, and her eyes finally closed. She knew she wasn't yet asleep, but she wasn't quite awake either. She was hovering in that curious limbo between the two and would have fallen fully asleep had she not been brought sharply back into consciousness by a voice.

"What are you doing here?" the man asked, holding an oil lamp aloft and squinting old eyes at her.

"I just came in to sit for a little while, sir," Violet said, nauseated by the shock of being suddenly awoken. "Reverend, I am in need of a little mercy."

The old Reverend smiled, but his eyes held a sadness in them. "Of course, my dear. We must strive to deal the same mercy that our God deals us."

"I'm so tired," Violet said, feeling an exhaustion that was bone-deep.

"You can stay here for tonight. I will remain awake and around, so you need not fear any intruders." The Reverend paused a moment before continuing. "But I am very sorry, for tomorrow morning you must be on your way. If we housed everyone in need of a place to stay indefinitely, well…" He trailed off, obvious guilt in his eyes.

"I understand." Violet was just grateful to have somewhere – anywhere – to stay for her first night of freedom.

"What has led you here, may I ask? For I must not only work as a helper, but also as a teacher. And if this has been brought on by a slothfulness in you—"

The man's words held no accusation, but Violet couldn't help but cut him off. "I have worked hard all my life, sir. I have worked until my fingers have bled and have never once asked for special consideration. I am running away from cruelty, and I ran into God's house looking for safety."

The Reverend nodding sadly. He clearly understood. Violet could tell she wasn't the first poor soul to come desperate and lost, due to the cruelty of others. Violet would have liked to continue their conversation, but her eye-lids were so heavy. She curled up in a ball to sleep, with the Reverend – and God above – watching over. She would need to move on in the morning, but that was the morning's problem.

CHAPTER 8

It was a mercifully dry morning, although it was cold. The Reverend was kind enough to give her some water and a few slices of buttered bread before sending her on her way, stating she would be in his prayers. She wondered how many people would have to be in a Reverend's prayers.

She wandered aimlessly through the city streets for a time, not really sure what to do, other than to continue to get further and further away from Micah Turner. People hardly saw her as they bustled passed, and those that did normally stuck their noses up at the state she was in and the clothes she was wearing.

Eventually, she collapsed down in a deserted alleyway to catch her breath and rest. The sun was starting to set again, making all the shadows long, and the atmosphere gloomy. It wasn't long before there came the sound of shuffling, staggering footsteps. She peered down the alleyway, realising that the owner of the footsteps was coming towards her. Violet stayed still as a statue and hoped that the man, who must surely be drunk, wouldn't notice her there huddled by the threshold of a side door into the building she was currently leaning against.

She held her breath as the man dragged his feet, one after the other, slopping his way along the alleyway. He seemed to go right past her, even though she was certain that he'd seen her. She gave a sigh of relief until the footsteps stopped, and she heard the man cough. When the footstep started up again, Violet realised that they were coming back towards her.

"The very girl I was looking for!" he said in a horrible, slurred voice. She realised then that he had seen her the first time but hadn't quite registered her in his befuddled state until he stopped to clear his throat. If only he had kept walking.

"I think you must have me mistaken, sir."

"Oh, Miss hoity-toity!" he said and laughed. "Now cough up the money you owe me, and we'll calls all fair. Shan't we do that darlin'?" At least, that's what Violet thought he said. His words were so slurred it was hard to fully understand them all.

"You most definitely are mistaken, sir. I've never met you before, and I don't have any money. Even if I did, I wouldn't owe any of it to you. I'm just looking for somewhere to sleep. I have no place to sleep, but this, that's all," Violet said, realising she had nowhere to back away to, he more or less had her cornered without even trying.

"No money?" The man starred dumbly at her in his drunken haze. The pause was terrifying. "Well you'll just have to pay me in other ways. How's about a kiss for your old lover, eh? Just like old times my Bettie."

He pounced on her with surprising accuracy, given his level of drunkenness, and she could smell the awful liquor on his breath as he tried to kiss her. Violet twisted her head this way and that.

"No! I said, no! Get off me! I am not Bettie!" She was yelling now, kicking and struggling. "Please! Help! Anyone! Help!"

The man was now most intent, hardly even registering her screams and pleas for mercy. He was so intent, in fact, that he didn't see a woman approaching in the darkness of the alleyway, nor did he see when she raised her arm aloft, and the glass of the empty gin bottle. In fact, the first he knew of it was that handful of tiny moments from the time that the bottle had hit him on the side of the head with a dreadful thump until the moment that he slid into unconsciousness.

The woman, young, pretty, and with a head full of wild

blonde curls, used her booted foot to roll the sailor off Violet.

"Stupid fool," the girl said and laughed. She had a surprisingly deep voice for one so pretty. "Even a drunken sailor can see that you're no prostitute!" She reached down, holding out a hand to Violet.

Violet took her hand gratefully, and the woman pulled her to her feet. She could see her taking in her appearance, the striped dress, the unmistakable uniform of the workhouse. "I don't think he thought I was a prostitute,,," Violet said as she was pulled up. "He thought I was some old lover named Bettie? Who owed him money apparently."

"That the story he spin you ay?" Lily looked down and gently nudged the unconscious man with the tip of her shoe. "Always something with these ones." Her bright eyes flicked back up to Violet. "I'm Lily. Lily Clark," she said, that deep voice still so surprising.

"I'm Violet Marsh. Thank you for helping me. If you hadn't come along, I don't know what I would have done."

"You'd have been in a right state, that's what!" she said and chuckled. "Come on, I can't leave a girl like you in a place like this, can I? That's the problem with sleeping in an alleyway so close to the river, pet, every drunken idiot who staggers past is certain they know you, and also certain you owe 'em something or other. Well, let's at least get you out of harm's way for tonight. I'm in no mood to pick up any more fellows, time to turn in." She held out her arm, and Violet took it.

"Pick up any more fellows?"

"Well, bless me, ain't you a sheltered one. Let me guess, lived in the workhouse your whole life? From a baby?"

"Yes, I think so."

"Well, let me begin your education right now, pet. You might not be a prostitute, but I am. If I wasn't, I'd be a starved-to-death bag of bones lying in this alley. Since that's something I'm not prepared to be, I do what I can."

"Of course," Violet said and nodded, neither smiling nor wincing. The woman had helped her, and she was in no position to judge even if she hadn't.

"Well, sheltered you might be, but I reckon snooty you ain't. Come on, you can come to my room. You can tell me all about it." She grinned, and the two of them set off into the night. Without knowing if she really was safe, Violet thought that this was certainly as close to it as she was going to get that night, at any rate.

Lily Clark lived in a single room on the ground floor of a rundown terraced house. It was one of the small terraces, low and pitiful looking. The brickwork was blackened, a by-product of this industrial age. It was so black, in fact, that it could be easily seen to be so even just by moonlight.

The back door of the terraced house was accessed via a little alley at the back, which led into a tiny square flagstoned yard. The door didn't open directly into Lily's room, but rather a small room with a stone sink with a cold-water tap, and a mangle set on a small wooden table.

"Oh, yes, it's very modern here. Apart from the mould, the rats, and the wind howling in through the window frames, the landlord does at least provide us with running cold water. I suppose that's why he feels free to put the rent up whenever he likes," Lily said, and sounded a little bitter.

When Lily led her into her room, at last, Violet's eyes almost flew wide at the state of the place. It wasn't just the landlord's dereliction of duty in terms of maintenance, but a little of Lily's own slovenliness. There were dresses strewn about the place, a bowl with the remnants of some stew or other sitting on the floor by the bed. Oh, and the bed looked truly awful. It was a wide bed, not one of the little tiny ones that she had slept on in the workhouse. This one was big enough for two people.

"You can sleep with me tonight, pet. You'll feel better once you've had a good night's sleep," Lily said happily, hardly seeming to realise the state of her own lodgings.

"Thank you, Lily. You've been so kind to me." It was all Violet could think of to say. It was the truth, of course, but she'd spoken it hurriedly so that Lily wouldn't realise her shock at the state of things.

The workhouse was an awful place, but the inmates were truly worked to the bone, including keeping the place clean and orderly. Violet had never had any true idea of how people lived outside, and she wondered if this was simply normal.

"I haven't got a nightgown to give you, pet, I don't tend to sleep in one, if you know what I mean," Lily grinned again.

Violet smiled shyly back, hoping that her blushes couldn't be seen by the pale yellow light of two slim candles that Lily had left burning.

"I brought mine with me." Violet reached into the front of her shift dress and pulled out the nightgown she had stowed there earlier.

"Clever girl. Just a pity you didn't come away with a little of the workhouse silver!" She let out a deep, booming laugh, and Violet, feeling safe even if she was just a little perturbed by the dirty surroundings, relaxed enough to join her in her laughter.

"So, what's your story then? If you had to leave the workhouse, why didn't they give you your clothes back?"

"I never did have my own clothes, Lily. Like you said, I've been there since I was a little child."

"Oh, yes, of course. Well, we'll have to see what we can find you. Can't have you wondering about the place in that awful striped thing, can we?"

"Thank you," Violet said, and secretly hoped that whatever dress Lily found her wouldn't be quite as low-cut and as tight as the one that Lily was wearing.

"Why did you leave? Throw you out, did they?"

"I had to leave. I had to run," Violet said, deciding to be completely honest with the woman who had saved her.

"Why?" Lily asked as she unashamedly stripped down to nakedness and climbed into the bed.

"I was almost attacked."

"I've heard there are some rough women in there, all right!"

"No, it wasn't one of the women. It wasn't one of the inmates, Lily. It was a man who works there," she said and decided not to tell her exactly who it was. "And it wasn't an attack exactly... He's an awful man, a terrible man. He's done the same thing to other girls in the workhouse, and there's one he's treated so badly that he's driven her to insanity. I had to run, he's such a bad man."

"A bad man, yes, he sounds like he is just that. Most of them are, pet. He's just a bad man in amongst a world full of bad men." Lily closed her eyes and pulled her blankets up around her before adding rather ambiguously, "You'll get used to them."

Lily seemed to fall asleep immediately, and as Violet hurriedly changed into her nightgown and climbed in beside her, she wondered just exactly what Lily had meant.

CHAPTER 9

Violet had been with Lily for just a few days, but already she liked her very much. Perhaps it was because she had rescued her, and perhaps it was because she recognised something in the young woman's helpless situation. Although she had lived in the workhouse as long as she could remember, there was a strange sort of system of education whereby young girls picked up the details of the seedier modes of living in conversation with the older women who didn't always stay for long at the workhouse but seemed to be regular visitors. They were ones who had lived those lives, who knew what it was to struggle and then be forced to give in and tap once again at the workhouse door.

Violet knew full well that there were women in the world who had no choice but to sell their bodies to ugly, grubby men. Without Lily to look after her, she might well have had to make the same decision herself, she could see that quite clearly now. But it wasn't the way she wanted her life to go, she didn't even want to think about it. For now, she was safe. For now, she wanted to find a way to have Lily see her as somebody she wanted to keep around. So, when Lily had gone out in the late afternoon, declaring that she would be able to pick up a few bits and pieces cheaper at the market at the end of the day, Violet set about making herself useful.

In no time at all, she had tidied away Lily's clothes, folding them neatly and piling them on an old chair in the corner of the room. There were no cupboards to speak of, but she could at least find a way, a system, of keeping things tidy.

She collected the dirty bowls from the floor, and a plate filled with dried crumbs from some bread that the two of them had eaten the day before. There was no sense in encouraging rats, after all, was there?

Violet ventured out into that little room beyond, the room with the stone sink, and was pleased to find a broom, a bucket, and some scrubbing brushes. It wouldn't be the first time that she had not only scrubbed floors with cold water alone but had done a good job of it.

Once the floor was clean, Violet cleaned the burnt coals and ash from the fire grate and wiped everything down. She cleaned the little metal tripod and scrubbed the one saucepan which hung from it. She scrubbed the plate, the two little bowls, and the spoons. She stacked them neatly on the window ledge before she wiped down every shelf and surface, dispelling the dust.

It was a warm enough day, although not yet summer, and she opened the window to allow a little fresh air inside. Finally, she made the bed. It was something she'd had to do every day of her life back at the workhouse, and it seemed somehow strange to her that it was something Lily *never* bothered to do. She simply climbed out and left the sheets and blankets wherever it was they landed.

It was too late in the day to wash the bedding and hang it out in the yard to dry, but Violet made a mental note to do just that the next day. If Lily got out of her bed early enough, Violet would get it stripped down and get it cleaned. She only hoped that Lily would be pleased rather than insulted.

By the time Lily returned, the sun was going down. She walked into the room with an armload of bits and pieces; half a loaf of bread which looked dry and hard, a few potatoes, carrots, and a bottle of gin.

"Have I come back to the right house?" Lily asked, and that deep voice boomed with laughter. "Well now, haven't you been making yourself busy!"

"I hope you don't mind, Lily? I just wanted to do something to say thank you."

"You help yourself, pet. If that's what takes your fancy, don't you mind me."

"I could make some soup with those vegetables if you like?"

"You're turning out to be a proper little treasure, aren't you?" Lily said and smiled as Violet relieved her of her purchases. "I reckon we'll need a bit of soup to dip this bread in. It's far too hard to attempt without softening it up a bit."

As Violet set about cutting the vegetables and adding a little water to them, then setting the fire and lighting it, Lily sat on the end of her bed and drank the gin straight from the bottle. It wasn't the first time that Violet had seen her do it, and already the sight had become so commonplace it was no longer shocking.

"Here, have some," Lily said and held out the bottle. "You've earned it, pet."

Violet understood entirely now why Lily drank. She swallowed down that gin to dull the pain of her life, and it made Violet feel sad. Violet's own life had been far from happy, but she knew it wasn't so bad that she needed to drink it away. Not to mention the fact that gin had been denounced as the work of the devil so many times by Vera Packham that Violet was simply too afraid to take even one swallow.

"No, thank you, Lily. I don't know, I've never really liked the taste," Violet said, lying, not wanting to offend Lily or to seem to be judging her. "I just can't get it down me." She gave a self-deprecating laugh.

"You don't know what you're missing!" Lily said and laughed before taking another swig. "Well, I suppose it's all the more for me."

"Apparently, every cloud has a silver lining."

"And so it does!" Lily said and laughed again.

Violet let out a laugh more rich and true than any she had ever heard. For the first time in a long time, she was out in that wonderful park again, a little girl in a pretty blue silk dress with a cream bow, her arm stretched high above her as she held onto the warm, smooth hand of the woman she was so certain was her mother.

The day was warm and bright, the sun was high in the bright blue sky. It was the same in every detail, everything just as she had always remembered it. But wait... There was something new! On the other side of her, holding her other hand, was her childhood friend, Joe Willis. He was still just eight years old, never having changed a bit. But of course, he wouldn't have, would he? Dead children don't grow old, do they?

It was at this moment that Violet woke up. She wiped a tear from her eye. Her heart ached whenever she thought about Joe. She missed him so much.

She raised her head silently to check on Lily. After it became apparent that Violet would be staying for a while, a small bed of sorts – made out of various blankets and clothes – had been set up in the far corner of the room, allowing for some sense of privacy, although Lily hadn't seemed to mind sharing.

Even from a quick glance Violet could tell that Lily was in fact still sharing her bed, with one of her customers no doubt. Violet had thankfully been asleep whenever the two of them had entered.

Violet set her head down on her not quite comfortable pillow again. With tears rolling down her face, the comfort of her mind's eye imaginings now completely ruined, Violet wished that her life was different. She wished all their lives were different. Just as she had told Millie, she didn't believe that anybody was meant to live this way.

CHAPTER 10

"Work? What sort of work? You're not thinking of going back into the workhouse, are you?" Lily asked and seemed utterly bemused.

"Any kind of work, Lily. I've been here for months now, and it isn't fair on you. I'm sixteen now, I should be working. I just want to earn some money so that I can help out."

"Well, that certainly is very good of you, pet, I just don't know what sort of work you're talking about."

"Anything. I just don't want you to have to take all the strain, and it can't be easy having an extra mouth to feed." Violet knew that she didn't really cost much at all. The food they shared was simple and cheap, and she still hadn't taken a single drop of gin. That was a road she didn't want to set a single toe on for fear of where it would lead her.

"But what sort of thing? You must have thought of something." Lily didn't seem as enthusiastic as she had imagined she would.

"Maybe I could try one of the nice-looking houses and see if they need a scullery maid. I can do cooking and cleaning, anything like that. We were trained at the workhouse to be ready for a position in service when we finally came back out into the world. I know how to grow vegetables too, that was one of my jobs." Violet smiled, but she couldn't help feeling a little crestfallen.

"My pet, do you really want to be working your fingers to the bone for hours on end and have very little to show for it?"

"It will be better than nothing, though, Lily. Even if it's only a few shillings a week, I would at least be able to buy the food and help with the rent, wouldn't I?"

"You really are a sweet girl, Violet. Now, I tell you this for your own good, pet," Lily said, looking suddenly a little furtive. "There are easier ways to make money. There are easier ways than fetching and carrying for folks who are too lazy to do it for themselves."

"You mean...?" Violet just couldn't say it out loud.

"It's good enough for me, but isn't good enough for you? Is that what you're saying?" It was the closest the two had ever come to falling out, and Violet's eyes immediately filled with tears.

"No, that's not what I'm saying. I'd never say that about you, Lily."

"Now, don't cry, pet, I didn't mean to be so snappy. Go on then, if you're so determined to scrub floors for people, then that's what you must do." Lily wrapped her arms around Violet and pulled her in close. She kissed the top of her head. "Don't you mind me. I'll be better when I've had a few gulps of my medicine now, won't I?"

Lily released her and walked across the room, taking the gin bottle from the windowsill and having several noisy gulps. *Her medicine.* It made Violet so sad. If only she could persuade Lily to do the same, to just work in service. If she did, then between them, they would surely have enough money to keep that room and live a decent sort of life. Still, that would be an argument for another day.

It was autumn now, and the day was chilly but bright as she made her way along to Kennington Road, where there were a few more respectable looking dwellings. They were still terraced houses, but they were the tall ones with long sash windows. They weren't the wealthiest places in London, but they housed the sort of families who could afford one or two poorly paid servants. Violet felt confident; with her experience, surely, she would find herself something suitable.

When she arrived at the first of the terraces, she made her way around the back and down to the servants' entrance. She knocked tentatively at the door, and it was opened by a short, rotund woman in her late forties. There was something familiar about her, and Violet wondered if she had seen her about the town or the market.

"Yes?" the woman asked and narrowed her eyes, looking Violet up and down.

"Good morning. Forgive me, but I'm looking for work in service. I have some experience, I'm a hard worker. I can clean, do laundry, and I can prepare vegetables. I can even cook."

"Well, well, isn't that quite the list of accomplishments!" the woman said sarcastically.

Her face was round, and the colour in her cheeks was high. Once again, she looked Violet up and down, and it was clear that she recognised her also. Violet tried to smile, but she was far too nervous to manage something so simple and be anything like convincing.

"I'm prepared to do anything, I'm a hard worker."

"Oh, yes, I'll just bet you're prepared to do *anything*. Absolutely anything. In fact, I'll dare bet that you are already doing just about *anything* for money." The woman looked so scornful that Violet almost withered under her scrutiny.

"I beg your pardon?" Violet said, the beginnings of understanding starting to claw at the edge of her mind.

"Don't look so innocent with me, I know what you are."

"What I am?"

"Never mind staring at me with big doe eyes, girl, as I said, I know what you are. Now, my mistress isn't the richest of women, but she's respectable enough that she wouldn't have your sort working here. I can't believe you're even standing there expecting it!"

"I don't understand," Violet said, but she did. She just didn't want to admit it, to acknowledge it, to let it be real.

"Don't even think about telling me that you live in that rotten little room with Lily Clark, the busiest harlot in town, and declare that you don't do just the same as she does. You shouldn't be knocking on the doors of decent folk, not one of your sort. You've made your choices! You can't just go switching to something clean and decent when you feel like it."

"I've never done that in my life, not once. And it's hard of you to go judging Lily when she doesn't have a choice."

"We all have choices."

"But we don't, do we? You just said it yourself!" Violet was becoming angry, even though she knew it wouldn't help her cause. "You've just said that she would never be able to switch to something decent, didn't you? So how does she have a choice at all anymore?"

"That you would stand here outside a house of respectability and start shouting the odds, defending your hussy of a friend! What sort of girl does that? How can you defend her? I'll tell you how!" She folded her arms across her ample bosom and glared. "You can defend a harlot because you *are* one. A clean and decent girl would not be able to get the words out. Now get away with you!"

"You might think yourself respectable, but at least Lily Clark has a heart in her chest." And with that, Violet slowly walked away.

Utterly crestfallen and a little shaken, she leaned against a wrought iron lamp post for a moment and tried to control her breathing. She wasn't going to be put off so easily. That horrible woman might well have recognised her, but perhaps she would be lucky at the next house.

However, by the time she had made her way to the next possibility, it seemed that the dumpy red-faced woman had already made her way to every respectable house the full length of the terraces and warned them about her.

Violet was chased away from two houses, and when she tried at yet another, the door wasn't even opened to her. A gravelly female voice from within simply shouted through the window, "Get away, you little Jezebel!"

In tears, Violet hurried away from the house and crossed the street. There was a small square of green grass and a few trees neatly enclosed by chest height wrought iron fencing. She pushed open the gate and walked inside, quickly finding a little bench and sitting down on it. Drawing her handkerchief from the sleeve of her dress, she hurriedly dried her eyes.

"Are you the one who's looking for work?" A rough-looking man had followed her through the gate and was now standing before her, looking down at her.

"I'm not what you think I am, so get away from me!"

"Steady on, love!" he said and started to laugh. It was an amused laugh rather than a cruel one, and she didn't feel quite as threatened as she ordinarily might. "I don't care what you are as long as you're looking to work hard."

"As what?" Violet asked, in no mood to be propositioned.

"My name is Stan," he said and held out his hand. Violet took it, although she wasn't at all sure that she should. Still, he only gently shook it and then released her. "I'm always looking for kids to go out collecting for me."

"I'm sixteen, I'm not a kid."

"You're still young, love!" he said and laughed again.

"Collecting what?"

"Pure. You know what that is, don't you?"

"Yes," she said and shuddered visibly, making him laugh again. She really did wish she hadn't shaken his hand now. Of course, he probably didn't handle much of the pure himself, leaving it to poor young children to do the dirty work.

Pure was a rather pleasant name given to the most unpleasant substance. It was, in fact, dog faeces. It was collected from the street and sold to tanners, who used it in the treatment of new leather.

"What's the matter? Not good enough for you?" he said, still smiling at her pleasantly. "If you work at it, you'll earn a few shillings. I don't want to be the one to point it out to you, but Vera Thistlethwaite has a big gob, she'll have already warned half of London not to employ you."

"Vera? Her name is Vera, is it?" Violet shook her head. "I suppose I shouldn't be surprised by that."

"To be honest, love, I've got no idea what you're talking about. So, you want to earn yourself a few shillings or not? Come on, I haven't got all day."

"Yes, all right." She got to her feet. "Thank you," she added, thinking that it was probably best that she shows some appreciation, even if she had just accepted the worst job in the world.

However, as she walked along at Stan's side, she knew it wasn't the worst job in the world. It couldn't be any other than the *second* worst job in the world, for she knew precisely what the worst was. And in the end, it all boiled down to one simple question. Would she rather do this than earn her living the way that Lily Clark did? And the answer was *yes*, of course, it was yes. As foul and demeaning as this job undoubtedly would be, to prostitute herself would be far worse.

How she wished that Micah Turner hadn't made it impossible for her to stay at the workhouse. If she had stayed, she would still be learning the ropes of what it would mean to be in service. She might even have been found a position somewhere by now, or certainly not far from now. She might have come from the workhouse, but she would certainly have been seen as more respectable than she was seen now.

It didn't matter that she had never worked as a prostitute, the awful Vera Thistlethwaite would certainly see to it that everybody was convinced that she had. She would never get a job in service now, not in this part of town. She was no longer respectable, even though she'd done nothing to deserve it.

At that moment, she felt terrible. She felt guilty; she was doing what everybody else did in deciding who did and did not deserve respect. She knew that Lily didn't have a choice, and she knew it now more certainly than ever. As long as there were people like Vera Thistlethwaite in the world, Lily would be trapped forever.

So, if she had to pick up a little dog mess, then who was Violet to complain about it?

CHAPTER 11

Violet could hardly believe she had only been out on Vauxhall Walk for an hour. The smell emanating from the tin bucket Stan had given her was so foul that she wondered how she would get through the day. It made her think that even a day spent oakum picking used to go along a little faster than the day did now.

It had taken her a little while to train her eyes to be able to distinguish the little mounds of dog faeces in amongst so much horse manure, but she was getting the hang of it. Still, it was an awful way to make a few coins, and even though Stan had given her a single glove, still, she felt she would never be clean again. And the glove was almost worthless, being a left rather than a right. She had tried to pick up with her left hand but found it slowed her down too much. So, she'd had to put it on back to front on her right hand, and it felt tight and extremely awkward.

Nonetheless, she would persist in wearing it, even though two little girls she had seen with identical buckets to her own didn't seem to bother with such niceties, simply picking the foul mess up with their bare fingers.

The nearer she drew to the Vauxhall Pleasure Gardens, the more dog mess there was to be found. Unfortunately, she had to wade through the increasing amount of horse manure to get to it. It seemed there were to be no bright corners in her new occupation.

"Look at you, picking up the dog's doings!" came a loud and raucous shout. It was a voice Violet didn't recognise, and she wasn't at all surprised to see a drunken man wandering along towards her, amusing himself at her plight.

"There's better ways to make a coin, girl. Didn't anyone ever tell you that?" he said and raised the battered old top hat he'd clearly either stolen or been given in an act of curious charity. It looked so incongruous against the ragged, poorly made old trousers and jacket he was wearing, almost as if he had been wearing it as a joke.

"Go away," Violet said and looked back down into the mess of the road.

"Pretty girl like you would make a pretty penny too. And you look clean, even though you're picking that lot up!" he said and boomed with drunken laughter.

"Mind your own business and leave me alone."

"Why?"

"Because she asked you to, that's why!" Another man had appeared on the scene, only this man was a gentleman.

"Oh, I didn't mean nothing by it. I didn't mean no offence, sir." He lifted his top hat and bowed, making his apology to the gentleman rather than to Violet, the one he had offended. It wasn't lost on her, and Violet slowly rose to her feet, holding onto her tin bucket.

"Then perhaps you should be on your way," the gentleman went on, clearly not intending to leave her until he was sure she was safe. It worked, for the man touched the brim of his battered top hat and staggered away.

"Thank you, sir," Violet said, feeling very awkward; she'd never spoken to a gentleman before.

"He is something of a nuisance in the Pleasure Gardens. Harmless enough, but he ought not to have pestered you." The man was tall and upright, with hair that would have been the same colour as her own had it not been liberally sprinkled with thick grey strands.

He wore a fine suit of black trousers, smart shoes, and a waistcoat over his white shirt. His coat was black, and as fine a coat as she had ever seen close up. He wore a black hat, although not quite as large as the top hat the drunken man had worn.

Violet didn't know what else to say, for the man seemed to hesitate for a moment. He seemed to bite his bottom lip, and when Violet saw his eyes stray inevitably to the contents of her tin bucket, she knew that he was trying to hide his revulsion. He smiled at her, and somehow it made her feel worse.

He was trying to be kind, and it gave her the distinct impression that she was simply a figure to be pitied, so low that he didn't know how to extricate himself from the now-embarrassing little encounter. Finally, he dug into his trouser pocket and pulled out a small black leather purse.

Violet bowed her head. Even though she had been raised in the workhouse and reminded daily of the charity she was in receipt of, this was the first time she had been shown true charity. This was a man handing her some coins without any expectation that she worked for them. No oakum picking or pure collecting, just charity. She couldn't afford to turn it down, but it made her eyes swim with tears of shame.

"Thank you, sir," she said when he dropped the coins into her left, un-gloved, and clean hand.

"Take care, child," he said and nodded briefly before turning to take his leave.

As he walked along Vauxhall Walk, his cane tapping the ground intermittently as he went, Violet stared after him, tears streaming down her face.

"Oh my! I can smell you for miles!" Lily said when Violet returned home after her first day.

"Can you really?" Violet asked, mortified.

"I'm just teasing you. It's not so bad, but I can smell it a bit. You need to be more careful about that dress."

"I'll wash it tonight and use my old workhouse dress for work in the future," Violet said.

"Work? So, you're not put off by your first day, then?" Lily was laughing, but it was kindly.

"No," Violet said without conviction. "And here," she went on with a smile when she handed Lily the coins she'd earned for the day. She kept the coins the gentleman had given her in the pocket of her dress. That wasn't earnings, after all, it had been a gift. Well, charity.

"Is that all?" Lily said, her mouth wide open in surprise. "Oh, I'm sorry, pet. Thank you, I do appreciate it. It just seems so little to be out all day picking up that foul-smelling mess. How long were you at it? Eight hours? Nine?"

"Thereabouts."

"Oh, Violet, I wish you'd listen to me. I know you don't want to do it, but you'd earn that in a couple of hours," Lily said, staring down at the coins in her hand.

"I'll be all right, Lily. And I'll probably get better at it, faster, so I will soon be earning a little more than this."

"Even if you earned twice as much, I can promise you that it ain't worth it. Why do you want to make life so hard for yourself?"

"Maybe something else will come along," Violet said, not wanting to discuss this subject again. She couldn't tell Lily how opposed she was to prostitution without offending her, and she cared about her too much for that, not to mention her gratitude.

"Like what? Maybe you could go up in the world and sell watercress."

"Watercress?" Violet said, thinking how it would be preferable to collecting pure.

"Don't get your hopes up, I was just teasing you. Watercress sellers make about half what pure collectors make. Honestly, Vi, why do you think I'd rather do what I do?"

Violet didn't answer. She didn't have a good rebuttal, and Lily could see that.

"You'll learn, pet. You do what you have to do, my sweet. I think you'll have to suffer first before you come to your senses. You're a stubborn one, I'll give you that!" Lily laughed and reached for her shawl. The sun was going down, and Lily's workday was just about to begin. "Goodnight, pet," she went on, kissing the top of Violet's head. "Goodness, you do, stink!" She laughed, and so did Violet.

However, when Lily went out into the night, Violet's smile faded, and tears sprang to her eyes. Hardly knowing which part of her day had been the worst, she broke down into chest-tearing sobs, collapsing onto the scrubbed wooden floorboards and crying for all she was worth.

CHAPTER 12

Violet had been working all week collecting pure. But that first week had felt like a year, and she wondered if she would have to spend the rest of her life doing this.

It had been a long day, but it was her best yet. As she made her way back along Vauxhall Walk towards the Albert Embankment, where Stan sat in his cart at the end of each day to collect the buckets, she felt strangely pleased with herself. It had been her best day yet, and she had filled no less than two buckets.

However, her day was not to end well, and as she turned down Randall Row, she was hit hard between the shoulder blades. Violet cried out in surprise and dropped her buckets. One landed upright, but the second tipped over, spilling much of its contents on the road.

"You'll have to pick that lot up!" It was a girl's voice, and Violet spun around to see two girls behind her.

"Who hit me? Was it you?" she said to the taller of the two girls, the one who was glaring at her.

"That's what you get for stealing my pure!" the girl said, and then spat at her. Suddenly, Violet began to feel truly afraid, it was a curiously violent act, and the girl looked rough and nasty.

"Stealing? What are you talking about? I collected this, all of it." She looked down and could see that neither of the girls had buckets with them. She felt sick with suspicion; they meant to take her buckets from her.

"Who told you that you could work on my patch? I do Vauxhall Walk, always have." The same girl was speaking, with the smaller one nodding and glaring in support of her friend.

"But I've been there all week, and I never saw you once. Stan told me to go wherever I could find the stuff."

"Well, he should have told you to steer clear of Vauxhall Walk."

"I'll go somewhere else tomorrow," Violet said, hoping that a little co-operation would save her. She crouched down, ready to put the pure back into the bucket.

"You'll have to give the buckets to us. As I said, that's my pure, not yours." The girl wasn't going to give in.

"No, it's mine. I worked for it."

"*I worked for it!*" the girl said in a whiny imitation of Violet. "Get her!" she hissed, and the two girls each grabbed a handful of Violet's hair, dragging her back into the adjacent park, a small pocket of grass known as Pedlar's Park.

Violet cried out in pain, but there was nobody in the park. The girls pulled at her mercilessly, and Violet held onto her scalp, trying to put an end to the searing pain. Finally, the girls let go, and she was about to catch her breath when they began to kick her. Their boots were hard, and they attacked her like a pack of dogs.

When it seemed that they would never stop kicking, Violet closed her eyes, stopped defending herself, and feigned unconsciousness. After just a couple more kicks, the girls stopped and fell silent. For the first time, she heard the smaller girl speak.

"We've killed her!"

"Don't be so stupid. She ain't dead, she's just fainted or something." Violet remained as still as a statue, even though she was in so much pain.

"She's dead," the little one persisted.

"She ain't!" But the girl sounded less sure of herself now.

"We'll hang if she is!"

"No, we won't. Let's just leave her here. Who will even know it was us? If she's dead, she can't tell, can she?" The uncertainty was gone, as was the humanity, as the taller girl convinced herself that she would be in no trouble at all. "Just grab the buckets, and we'll go over to Stan before he drives his cart away. Come on!"

Even though they were stealing her whole day's earnings, Violet kept her eyes closed until she was sure they had gone.

"So, what did Stan say?" Lily asked as she dabbed at Violet's bleeding scalp with a damp cloth.

"That it wasn't his fault I was robbed. He'd paid for the pure once, and he wasn't about to pay for it again."

"I suppose I could have guessed that much," Lily said with a sigh.

"He didn't care, even though I know he knows which girls did it."

"Nobody cares, pet. As long as they have enough money to survive, they don't give a toss about those who made it for them. How many more times do I have to tell you this?" Although she was taking care of her, there was a distinct note of exasperation in Lily's voice.

"I'm sorry. I won't let it happen again." It would have been the best money Violet had brought home all week, and the injustice of it all burned worse than her bloodied scalp.

"You might as well leave that bowl of water out; you never know what state I'm going to come back in tonight," Lily sounded hard suddenly as she tossed the cloth into the bowl of water.

She got herself ready for the night ahead without a word, only pausing now and again to take deep swigs from the gin bottle. Violet felt sick as she watched her, praying that she would find her usual humour any moment and tell her she was just teasing her. But the comment about her potential need to have her own injuries looked at after a night on the streets wasn't lost on Violet.

My life is harder than yours. That was the insinuation. *I suffer the most and bring in the most money.* It was clear, so very clear. It was also true.

"I'm sorry, Lily. I'll leave you in peace for now," Violet said cautiously and got to her feet.

"You ain't going anywhere, pet. It's time you learned a lesson or two about life, starting right now." Lily had the most determined look on her face, so determined that she was no longer pretty. Instead, she looked rough and hard-faced, every bit the work-weary prostitute. "You're coming out with me."

"What do you mean?" Violet asked and felt as suspicious and unsafe as she had when the two vile girls had approached her.

"You know what I mean," Lily snapped.

"What? No!" Violet cried.

"Even if I have to hold you down myself for the first couple times! I will teach you how to make it in this cruel nasty world!" Lily's voice raised, and the stench of gin seemed to permeate out of every pore in her body.

"What's wrong with you? You know I don't want to! You know I ran from the workhouse because someone was going to force me. How could you even think about holding me down whilst..." Violet couldn't finish the sentence. She was shaking and crying, but more murderously angry than she had ever been in her life.

"Why? Because you wouldn't listen, would you? You're so high and mighty! You think yourself too good to do what I do! Well, if I'd known that at the time, I'd have left you in the alleyway. I'd have let him show you what it was all about! That's how I learnt. I didn't have anyone swoop in and give me some 'time to think about it'. I had to just accept my lot instantly." Lily's voice cracked with the pain of lost innocence.

"Is that why you helped me?" Violet said, realisation beginning to dawn on her; had she been gullible? Had she really been so utterly naïve? "You thought I'd eventually agree to this?"

"Who do you think you are?" Lily was yelling, and Violet could hardly believe what was happening. "I gave you plenty of time here to get used to the idea, even though you were plenty old enough to earn your keep."

"So, you gave me somewhere to stay because you thought you'd make money out of me sooner or later?"

"Well, look where that got me! Accepting a few coins made from selling a bucket of pure!"

"You were happy for me to clean this dirty room to clean that dirty bed! I've been tidying, scrubbing, cooking, and cleaning, mending your clothes and stockings. I suppose that suited you, did it?"

"It was the least you could do. The very least you could do to put your workhouse skills to good use. I still kept a roof over your head, and you're so selfish that you couldn't even take over now and give me a break."

"So that was the plan, was it?" Tears were streaming down Violet's face; she'd never felt so betrayed in all her life. "To keep me here, to make me feel grateful, and then to turn me out as a prostitute to make money for you. Tell me, would I still have been scrubbing the floor and washing your sheets?"

Lily shook her head bitterly. "I should have just walked away and left you there. You've been nothing but trouble!"

"Trouble? Well, at least I won't cause you any more problems, will I?" Violet picked up her nightgown and folded it neatly, tucking it down the front of her dress just as she had done all those months ago on the night she had escaped from the workhouse.

"What are you doing?" Lily asked and seemed suddenly sober.

Violet didn't answer immediately, she just wrapped her woollen shawl tighter around her shoulders and looked around the room for the last time.

"You're leaving?" Lily said, seeming shocked now.

"How is it that you think I can stay? After all that you've said?" Violet had no idea where she could go, she only knew that she couldn't stay there.

She was back to square one; it was as if the last months had never happened, and this was to be her first night out on the street after running from the workhouse.

"You just need time to…" Lily began, but Violet cut her off.

"Get used to the idea of being a prostitute? No, I won't. I am done with being forced by other people into what they believe is my lot in life. I ran from the workhouse to escape that, and I certainly won't stay here to end up right back where I started." As Violet walked to the door, Lily tried to stop her. She grabbed her arm, but Violet shook her off. Violet was furious and ready to fight for her life if she had to. She glared at Lily.

Lily backed away; her eyes were wide. She knew without a doubt that Violet would do whatever she had to do to get out of that room. She knew that Violet was going and that there was nothing she could do to stop her.

"Violet, please don't go," Lily said and began to cry.

"Take care of yourself, Lily," Violet replied, letting herself out. Before she closed the door behind her she added: "I'll keep you in my prayers, Lily. I promise."

CHAPTER 13

For some time, Violet wandered the streets looking for a safe alleyway in which to sleep. However, several of the alleys were already occupied by either drunks, prostitutes, or both, and the ones which weren't seemed strangely frightening for their deserted state. An alleyway wasn't a safe place to sleep, certainly not in that area, and so Violet determined to simply keep walking until daylight.

When the daylight came, Violet would once again try to look for work. There was no way that collecting pure was going to earn her enough to keep off the streets. Indeed, nothing but the very worst job in the world would be enough for her to find a room of her own. Service was the only option, for at least it might come with some sort of accommodation. However, for a position that came with a room, Violet would have to look elsewhere. The households which could afford help in that area weren't so wealthy that they had somewhere for their servants to live. Not to mention the fact that Vera Thistlethwaite had seen to it that nobody would employ her anyway due to her associations with Lily.

Nonetheless, she would never be able to rid herself of the gratitude she still felt for the fact that Lily had spared her that night and knocked the drunken man unconscious. Nothing was simple, was it? Not even hurt and betrayal. From the small moments, passing phrases and insights into Lily's life and upbringing, Violet knew Lily had been forced, shoved, and dragged into the life and attitude the woman now lived: a life of broken drunkenness – Violet would do her utmost not to end up down that same path.

Seeing the black water of the River Thames glinting in the moonlight, Violet found herself walking towards it. When she reached the embankment, she squinted in the darkness, staring over to London, which lay on the north of the river. Perhaps there was more to be had there, certainly in terms of opportunities. Who would know her there? Surely, Vera Thistlethwaite's gossip didn't reach that far, did it?

The truth was that Violet might just as well cross the river. There was nothing for her here now, unless she turned back and apologised to Lily, accepting her dreadful terms. No, she wouldn't. Just as in the workhouse, she would rather die. So, taking a deep breath, Violet Marsh began to walk towards the Westminster Bridge. She would cross the bridge and pray that it was worth the journey.

Although the streets seemed a little quieter, there being far fewer drunken shouts, scurrying feet, and other sounds which were abundant in the Lambeth area, still, Violet was afraid. It was still dark, and the unfamiliarity of her surroundings was unsettling. She felt like a stranger in a strange land, just by dint of the fact that she had crossed the river.

As she walked, she could see the beginnings of dawn. It would be an hour or two away yet, but there was something different now about the quality of the night sky that spoke of change, of the morning to come. Violet just kept walking, keeping to the shadows in the streets, which seemed to boast cleaner and bigger houses than there were south of the river. As she walked, she tried to imagine herself working inside one of them, living safely in a tiny room, stability at last.

Finally, she reached the edge of a park. Looking up and down the boundary, she realised that it was a huge park, far bigger than the little pocket parks in Lambeth. Surely, Pedlar's Park would have fit inside it several times over.

She took the path into the park, straining to see, determined not to walk into danger. She found a bench not too far into the park and thinking that it would be safer to stop there then keep going, she settled down on it and tried to sleep. Violet sat upright rather than lying down, not wanting to be found by the peelers and arrested for vagrancy. However, laying down or sitting up, she was too cold and afraid to have managed even a moment of sleep and instead, simply sat there waiting for morning to come.

As soon as it was light, Violet got up from the bench. She felt numb with the cold, trying not to think about what would happen to her if she didn't find a position soon. In the daylight, the park looked wonderful. It was still deserted, but it was a clean and pretty place. She walked through it now without any sense of fear; there was nobody here, no vagabonds lurking behind trees and bushes. Was this a different London?

There was a clear pathway through the park and a curiously shaped lake in the middle. The birds were beginning to wake, and despite feeling so cold and tired, Violet was strangely at peace. It was as if she had shaken off the dirt and grime of her old life, even though she didn't know what her new life would bring. She just kept walking; she just kept putting one foot in front of the other.

Almost an hour later, the sky was a pale, watery blue, the sunshine weak but comforting. Something about being in the park had restored her, had even made her start to feel optimistic. Violet knew that she had nothing to be optimistic about, but she didn't want to dwell on that. She didn't want to do anything to disrupt the little slice of peace.

Looking at the trees ahead, she could see a break in them, a wide road breaking through the parkland. She paused and drew in her breath; it felt familiar, it looked familiar. She turned off the path and wandered towards the thinning trees. She wanted to see that road.

The more she walked, the more familiar everything began to feel. Finally, she reached that wide road and knew that she would cross it. There was a park on the other side, although as she looked to her right, it dwindled away as very grand, very large homes took over. Feeling as if the world had slowed down around her, she slowly turned her head to look left and gasped when she saw the very thing which she had seen so many times in that wonderful, heart-warming, sad memory of hers. She saw the great house, the wonderful palace of her dreams.

"Of course," she said under her breath. "That must be Buckingham Palace. That must be the place where Queen Victoria lives!" Violet had been taught about the Queen and her various homes, of course. She never imagined that she would set eyes on Buckingham Palace for herself. Better still, she had never realised that she already had. Violet had been here before. Violet had seen this wide road and beautiful palace before.

She knew it was the exact place that she had once stood, that she had once walked hand-in-hand with the woman she had always been so certain was her mother. But where was her mother now? Why did she leave her all alone to suffer the way she had suffered her entire life? Had she really not wanted her? Had she really been a whore, her new-born child nothing but an inconvenience?

Violet shook her head; surely, that couldn't be right. She wasn't a baby when she'd ended up at the workhouse, she was sure of that now. Her memory of that day in that very park was of her as a small child, a child who could walk at her mother's side. She hadn't been a baby. That being the case, did any of the things the wardens at the workhouse had said to her over the years really ring true?

With tears streaming down her face, Violet simply kept walking. Even though she felt as if she had reached her destination, she knew that couldn't possibly be right. She couldn't stand there on that wide road forever staring down at the Palace of the Queen of England, could she?

CHAPTER 14

London was beginning to come to life, and Violet walked through the second, smaller park and kept going. She looked down at her dress, glad that she had been wearing the one that Lily had found her months before, and not the striped uniform shift dress of the workhouse. She certainly didn't look wealthy, not like some of the people she began to pass in the streets, but she didn't look so rough either. She was clean and decent, and her hair was still neatly pinned back, nothing to tell of her night spent out in the park and no obvious signs of the bruises which covered her body and scalp from the vicious beating.

She could hear shouts in the distance that felt familiar to her, and she wasn't at all surprised when she came upon a small market. There were wooden carts everywhere, with costermongers yelling in the same fashion they employed south of the river. Violet could smell bread, and her stomach began to rumble. She realised that she hadn't eaten since the previous morning. She was hardly able to reconcile the fact that so much had happened to her since then.

She had been robbed by the two vicious girls, her hair pulled, and her body kicked. Her ribs and back still ached, but she was glad that they hadn't marked her face. If she was to gain employment somewhere, surely, she wouldn't manage it if her face looked bruised or there was any sign of what she had suffered the day before.

Violet had been too upset and shaken to eat, and when Lily had returned home that evening, things had gone from bad to worse. How could all of that have happened in just one day? When her belly rumbled again, she knew she must have something to eat. But how? She didn't even have a coin in her pocket. She'd given all her prior earnings, such as they were, to Lily, and she'd earned nothing from the day before after her two buckets had been taken from her. As for the coins the kindly gentleman had given her, they were tucked behind a loose brick in the fireplace back in Lily's room.

As she walked around the edge of the market, Violet could see a costermonger's cart, which seemed to have been abandoned. Her eyes darted to and fro in search of the costermonger, but she could see nobody obvious. Being certain that she was not observed, Violet walked smartly past the cart, quickly thrusting out a hand to snatch a shining red apple as she went.

Still walking, trying to appear as if nothing had happened, she quickly stowed the apple into the pocket of her dress. She was so hungry, she could hardly wait until she was away from the market to eat the apple, but she knew she must. However, just as she turned into another street out of sight, she heard footsteps running behind her. Without looking back, Violet took to her heels. Somebody must have seen her, perhaps even the costermonger himself, and she knew she must escape. If he caught her, he would likely turn her into the peelers.

She ran harder than she'd ever run in her life, but her bruised ribs and back ached horribly, and she was so exhausted from a night without sleep that she couldn't maintain the speed. In no time at all, her arm was seized, and she knew that she was caught.

"I'm sorry, I'm sorry. I never stole anything in my life before, but I am so hungry." Violet was already crying, deciding that she could do no other than just tell the truth.

"All right, all right, don't go panicking!" The young man who still held her arm began to look concerned. "It's only an apple, I'm sorry, I didn't mean to frighten you." His face was young, and she realised that he was around her age, fifteen, perhaps sixteen.

"I know I shouldn't have taken it."

"Don't worry, just eat the apple, miss," he said, and then squinted, his face suddenly almost in hers as he studied her.

"I'm not a prostitute," Violet said in a sudden panic.

"I know," the young man said, and his eyes suddenly began to shine; he was emotional, she could see that, she just didn't understand it. "I know you're not a prostitute, Violet," he went on, and her mouth fell open.

"Joe?"

It really was Joe Willis, after more than eight years. Now that she knew it was him, now that the shock was beginning to subside, Violet wondered how it was she hadn't recognised him immediately. He'd grown into a handsome young man, but all the elements of his face which had made him a cheeky young boy were still there to be found if she looked hard enough.

He hadn't asked too many questions before holding out his arm and walking her away from the market. It hardly mattered to Violet where they were going, he was the one person in all the world she knew she could trust entirely.

"I'm going to take you to my room, Vi, it's not far from here. There's not much to it, but it's clean, and there's a bed, so you can rest for a little while. Sorry to cart you through the streets, you look exhausted, but I need to run back to my cart as soon as I can, otherwise there won't be a thing for me to go back to," he said and laughed.

"I can't believe it. I thought you were dead," Violet said in a far-off voice, her exhaustion was beginning to overwhelm her so much so that she didn't know how much further she could walk.

"I almost was, but that's a story for later. Come on, this is it," he said, leading her down the side of a tall terraced house, a far cry from the low, smoke-blackened building she had lived in with Lily.

It was on the ground floor, his room, but there the similarity to her previous dwelling ended. The room was at least twice the size of the one she had shared with Lily, and it was immaculately clean. She smiled to herself and almost laughed when she thought that the standards of workhouse children were so much higher. They have been trained to keep clean, to keep tidy, to easily look after themselves in the most fundamental way.

"Hopefully, the apple will keep you going for a little while, and there's the crusty end of a loaf on that shelf there. If I hadn't stuffed down all the cheese this morning, you might have had some, but I did, so you can't," he said, talking fast and grinning, reminding her so easily of the vibrant little boy he'd once been.

"Thank you, Joe. Thank you so much." Her voice was weak and distant.

"There's some water in that jug for drinking, and a little left in that other jug over there for washing if you want. But by the looks of you, that's the thing you need most right now," he said and pointed to the other side of the room where there was a bed. It was smaller than the bed at Lily's, being just big enough for one person. "Get yourself a good sleep, Violet, and I'll bring some decent food back with me this evening when I'm finished at the market. We'll talk then, all right?"

Violet nodded, her eyes filling with tears of gratitude. Seeing that Joe's eyes had similarly filled with tears, she reached out and touched his face. It seemed the little gesture was too much for him, and he finally and without warning pulled her into his arms and held her so tightly that she almost cried out; her ribs and back hurt terribly. Nonetheless, she stayed quiet, and when he finally released her, she would have given anything to have that extraordinary pain back if only to be in the arms of her best friend in the whole world.

CHAPTER 15

After the most beautiful, restful sleep Violet had enjoyed in living memory, she awoke feeling refreshed. It took a moment or two for her to realise where she was, that she was safe and that her beloved childhood friend was still alive. As everything came back to her, she sat up in bed, a broad smile spreading across her face and tears of happiness springing into her eyes. Whatever happened in life now, she could face it, whatever it was. She had Joe back, and they had always been able to weather any storm together.

It was late afternoon, and she was sure she would have a little while before Joe returned home. She got out of bed and poured water from the jug into the basin on a little wooden stand in the corner of the room. Violet gave herself a good wash, almost as if she was washing Lambeth out of her very pores. The bruises on her body were dark and angry, although she was certain that none of her ribs were broken. She dressed and then ran her fingers through her hair until it was smooth and tangle-free before re-pinning it into a neat bun at the back of her head. She felt alive, fresh, and she couldn't wait until Joe came home.

In the end, she hadn't even eaten the apple that she'd stolen, and it sat on the wooden table in the other corner of the room, a corner which Joe seemed to have set aside as a makeshift kitchen area. There were two plates and a bowl on the table, the remnants of the bread he had urged her to eat earlier, some spoons, and a knife. There was a clean saucepan, and she looked over to the fireplace, the embers of the fire he had set earlier dying away, but the well-used little metal rail telling her most exactly that he cooked for himself. He lived in a clean room, had a job, and kept himself neat and tidy and fed.

There came a gentle tap at the door before Joe gently opened it, and cautiously popped his head around the frame. He grinned at her, and she grinned back.

"Did you sleep?" he asked, coming into the room at last. "I didn't want to just blunder in. I didn't want to frighten you clean out of your skin."

"I did sleep, and I've been awake for a little while."

"And how do you feel?"

"Like a person again, Joe," she said and smiled.

"Eat that apple, for goodness sake. It will seem like a waste of my energetic running if it just sits there and goes brown," Joe said and laughed. "And that bread. Somebody needs to eat that bread whilst we've both still got our own teeth."

"I just fell asleep. I mean, I fell asleep straight away, but I will eat them."

"Just the apple, don't risk the bread now, I was just teasing. Anyway, I have this lot," he went on and reached into the inside pockets of his heavy mid-length coat and retrieved two potatoes, a carrot, a half a loaf of fresh bread, and what looked like a small piece of meat wrapped in paper. "I'll make you a stew out of this lot. I hope you still like rabbit!"

"Goodness, I can't remember the last time I ate a good meal like this," she said, staring at vegetables that were still in their prime and remembering how meagre the meals had been when Lily spent the vast majority of both their earnings on gin. "But I've been asleep all afternoon, and you've been hard at work, so I'm preparing it."

"No, I will."

"No, I will," she said, and they both burst out laughing. It was as if nothing had changed between them, as if seven years hadn't passed at all.

"All right, I give in, we'll work together," he said and shook himself out of his coat.

∼

"That stew was wonderful," Violet said, having spooned it down in no time.

"Here, there's still some bread left," Joe said and handed her a piece to mop up the juices still in the bottom of the bowl.

"Thank you. I was so, so hungry."

"Have you been out on the streets long?" he asked gently. "I mean, you don't look like you've slept on the streets at all, but how did you come to be in Piccadilly Circus?"

"Is that where I am?"

"No, this is Soho. Piccadilly Circus is where you pinched my apple! You didn't know where you were?"

"No, I crossed the river last night. I crossed Westminster Bridge, and I walked until I came into a park."

"St James's Park?"

"I don't know, it had a big pond in it, or a little lake, one of the other," she said and shrugged.

"Yes, that's St James'."

"And then I crossed over a wide road, and I looked to my left, and I saw it."

"Buckingham Palace." He nodded slowly. "When I saw it myself for the first time, I recognised it," he said and laughed. "I only went and recognised it from your old dream!"

"My legs nearly buckled when I saw it. It was the very place I remembered, the park, that wide road…"

"That's called the Mall."

"Is it? Well, I crossed over and went into another park, a smaller one. I don't know, I just wandered around in there for a little while and then I came out again and started walking through the streets. I lost all sense of direction, then I just kept going until I saw that market and stole the apple."

"It's a lot nicer than Lambeth, isn't it?"

"Yes, a lot nicer."

"So, what happened? Why were you crossing the river at night?"

"It's a long story, and I don't really know where to begin. I left the workhouse almost a year ago. I ran away, actually."

"What happened?" Joe asked, leaning his elbows on the table and smiling at her gently.

"It was awful after you left. I thought you were dead. That's what Millie said, anyway, and Micah Turner was so angry with you that day that I believed her. All I could think of was the day that he'd beaten you so hard, and I thought he must have done it again, only this time he didn't stop."

"You were there to stop him the first time, I still remember it." He reached out and touched her face as if the angry red welt of seven years ago was still there.

"I'd already moved into the girls' block, hadn't I, by the time you went?" she said, casting her mind back and remembering her pain of being separated from her friend.

"Yes, it was a pretty awful time, wasn't it?"

"The worst. Anyway, I suppose I survived it. Millie was hateful, picking on me all the time, but she was soon moved away into the women's block, and I just lost myself picking horrible little bits of rope and getting through each day. The years just wandered along." She was looking at Joe, but she wasn't really seeing him; she was staring into the past.

"What happened?"

"Micah Turner started to pay me some attention, Joe, the sort of attention that I didn't want."

"That doesn't surprise me. As soon as I moved up into the boys' block, I started to hear the rumours."

"And they were true. I mean, he didn't get me, not really, but I'm certain that he got Millie. She changed so much, she withered away to almost nothing. She pulled out almost all of her hair, and even though she was so awful to me, she didn't deserve that. He'd taken her reason, Joe. He'd taken her sanity."

"Just like he did my ma," Joe said, and his eyes filled with tears.

"You mean that's why…?"

"Yes. I found her, you know. I walked all the way to Croydon, to Cane Hill, and I saw her. Took me two days, it did. She didn't make much sense, but enough for me to know what had happened. Enough for me to know that if I ever get the chance to, I'll kill him with my bare hands. I know it's a sin, but I can't help it." Joe grinned, slightly embarrassed at his callousness.

"Where is she now?" Violet asked, tears running down her cheeks. "Is she still at Cane Hill?"

"No," he said and pointed upward, indicating heaven. "She died just a week after I saw her. I went back, and she was gone. Still, I know where she's buried, I make my way there now and again and leave her some flowers. In a post cart now, though. I don't walk it anymore."

"I'm so sorry, Joe."

"She's at peace now. There was never any coming back from what he did to her, I could see that in her eyes. It was a brave thing for you to do, to escape, and I reckon you saved your own sanity, if not your life."

"Well, I suppose I did, although I ended up in almost exactly the same position in the end."

"What happened?"

"On only my second night out on the streets, this drunken vagabond was giving me a lot of trouble. I was saved by a young woman, a prostitute called Lily. She was so kind, she let me share her room, and she seemed to be happy for me to just keep things clean and tidy and do the washing and the mending and the cooking. But in the end, she betrayed me. She only saved me that night so that she could turn me to prostitution a few months later so that I could keep her in gin."

"Oh, Vi," Joe said and closed his eyes.

"It didn't happen, Joe. That's why I'm here now. That's why I was wandering around hungry enough to steal an apple. Goodness, I can hardly believe it was just last night," she said, shaking her head. "She said some truly awful things, you see, she said she was quite prepared to hold me down for the first few times if need be… It was all said in the stupors of gin, but I couldn't trust her after that. She's… She's a very hurt woman, and I shall keep her in my prayers."

"You're so brave, Vi. You always were, even when we were little kids. You always do the right thing, even though you don't know what it's going to cost you. Like a smack across the face with a birch cane, you helped me anyway."

"As you helped me today."

"I told you we'd be free of that place one day, didn't I? That we'd be living the high life somewhere!" he said and laughed, breaking the little talk spell of the last few minutes.

"This really is the high life. This is such a nice room, Joe. You've done so well for yourself."

"That's another long story," he said and laughed. "I suppose I just want to hear about you right now."

"I think I've told you everything," she said and shrugged.

"Do you want anything else to eat? There's still some bread."

"No, thank you, I'm full now." She paused for a moment, thinking about the day Joe disappeared. Micah Turner had dragged him away, his face furious. But what had Joe been saying to her at the time? It was something about a secret, wasn't it?

"What's the matter? Are you scowling or thinking?" Joe asked and laughed.

"Thinking. Of course, thinking makes me scowl," Violet said, and Joe laughed all the harder. "Joe, do you remember that day? You came up to me as we were leaving the chapel after morning prayers. You were trying to tell me something, but then the Master dragged you away, and that was the last I saw of you."

"Yes, I remember that day."

"And do you remember what it was you were going to tell me? Didn't you say you'd found out some secret?"

"I had. But now that really is a long story, Vi, a story for another day."

"No, no!" Violet said and shook ahead vehemently. "Tell me now, Joe."

"You've waited seven years, what difference does one more day make?"

"Just tell me!" she said and reached out to gently pinch his arm, just as she might have done when they were children.

"All right, but we'll be talking late into the night, so be prepared for that!" he said and then took a deep breath.

CHAPTER 16

"In the middle of the night? You went wandering around the workhouse?! You knew how to take risks, didn't you?!" Violet said, sitting on the floor by the fire with Joe. She had a blanket around her shoulders as they shared a tin mug of hot tea between them.

"I was looking for my ma. Anyway, I ended up outside Micah Turner's office and heard him boasting to one of the wardens about something. He was drunk, I suppose that's what loosened his tongue. Anyway, I stood outside, hardly daring to breathe whilst I listened to him telling the warden that he was being paid off over and over again by a gentleman, a real gentleman called Oliver Daventry. When I heard your name mentioned, I knew I couldn't leave my hiding place until I'd heard it all."

"But what do I have to do with Oliver Daventry, whoever he is?"

"Oliver Daventry was a man with a secret. His daughter had given birth outside of wedlock, although she managed to keep her illegitimate child a secret from him for almost three years." Already, Violet's heart was beginning to pound.

"He found out?"

"Yes, he found out. She left the baby with an elderly woman in Mayfair. The old woman kept the child there, making up some story or other about the baby, I suppose. Anyway, Oliver Daventry's daughter could visit whenever she liked, and when the child was old enough to go out, she used to walk her in St James' Park and Green Park once a week. Her old man found out in the end, of course, and he had the child snatched in her sleep. He had a plan, you see. I suppose he must have known of Micah Turner and the way he flouted just about every regulation in the workhouse. He took the child to him, and Micah promised to hide her there, settling her into the children's block with a vague story about her mother being a prostitute who had abandoned her. Daventry didn't want to put the child in an orphanage, you see, because he was worried that his daughter would search the orphanages of London until she found her. His idea was that it wouldn't occur to her to go looking in the workhouses where children, even the orphans, generally begin life there with one or other of their parents. I suppose he thought it was the perfect plan. I suppose it was," Joe said and shrugged. "You all right, Violet?"

"Yes, I think so. I know it sounds as if I'm being stupid, I just want to be sure what you're saying." She paused, taking a sip of the hot tea. "Am I that baby? Was that really my mother walking me through the park all those years ago?"

"Yes, that was your mother. Esme Daventry, that's her name. Well, it was."

"Goodness, Micah Turner really did have his tongue loosened that night."

"No, I found that out afterwards. Once I'd escaped the workhouse, getting myself far, far away in case they found me, I made my way here. Well, I made my way to Mayfair first, but there was nothing doing there for me work-wise. I found myself in Piccadilly Circus, and I came to the notice of a kind old costermonger who took me on."

"You escaped? So, the Master knew that you'd overheard him?"

"I don't think he was sure until he saw me talking to you the next morning. I think he heard a little bit of what I said, and he just realised that I knew."

"He hurt you?"

"He'd only given me a little bit of a beating, to be honest. That's when he told the warden, the one he'd been boasting to the night before, to kill me. He handed the man a knife, and he told him to put it into my heart. The warden began to object, but Micah told him that they would just tell the authorities that they had found me dead, that I must have been killed in an argument with one of the other inmates."

"Oh, Joe! He really was going to kill you!"

"He didn't get the chance. Fortunately for me, the warden hesitated. He grabbed hold of me, but when he raised the knife, I could see he didn't have it in him. He released his grip just enough for me to break free, and I just charged past him. It was still broad daylight, and I ran, and I ran. Even now, I can't believe how many corridors the workhouse has. It has cupboards too, and I kept moving from one cupboard to another, hiding. I was in there all day, Vi. I could hear the two of them searching for me, footsteps, and whatnot. I just kept moving around until they gave up. I suppose they thought I'd already escaped, so I waited until it was dark, and I snuck out into the grounds and around the back. There was a door in the wall, an old wooden thing that was on its last legs."

"That's the same door I escaped from," Violet said and reached out to take his hand.

"Well, I got out of there, I can tell you. I crossed the river that night, and I just kept going. I eventually found myself in Piccadilly Circus, and the rest is sort of history really. I worked for this old costermonger, Bob Jones, right up until he died. He liked me, you know. I think he lost his own boy some years before, and he always said that my cheeky ways reminded him of his son."

"He sounds like a kind man."

"The kindest. He didn't like me sleeping on the streets, he said no child should have to do that. So, he made me up a little bed right here in this very room, in the corner there under the window. That's where I slept right up until he died last year."

"So, who do you work for now?"

"I don't work for anybody, Vi. Bob Jones had four carts, he used one, and then he let three other barrow boys take them. He'd have a little bit of the profit, you know. Nothing excessive, he let the blokes earn a living right enough. Anyway, he had a good bit of money behind him too, saved it away, he had. When he died, it broke my heart. He was like a real father to me." Joe looked sad, and Violet wondered just how much people like the two of them had to lose in life; it didn't seem fair. "He made a will though, old Bob. It all came to me, Vi. His little bit of money, certainly enough to keep me here in this room. His four carts as well, so I carry on running the one me and him used to work on all those years, and I keep renting out the other three. I've been very blessed, Violet."

"And you've worked hard, Joe."

"I have that," he said and chuckled.

"How did you know your ma had gone to Cane Hill?" Violet remembered Joe's mother hadn't been taken away until after he had gone.

"I just knew. I knew that that's where she'd end up, especially when our little interviews in the big room ended. When I wasn't there anymore. I told Bob about her, and he said I could make my way there if I wanted. He was even going to give me the money to go in one of the post carts, but I didn't want to take any more from him than I had already, so I walked all the way to Croydon. Sure enough, she was there."

"Did she recognise you?"

"Not until I was leaving. I mean, she told me all sorts of things, enough for me to piece it all together, but it was as if she'd been talking to somebody else altogether. It was only when I was walking away from the room that she called out after me. *"Goodbye, Joe."* And that was it." he said, and his voice broke. *"Goodbye, Joe."* He repeated. "It was as if she knew she'd never see me again. It was as if she knew she was dying, and this was her one and only chance to say goodbye to her little boy."

"I really am so sorry," Violet said and dried her eyes on her sleeve.

"She's at peace now. She's been at peace for more than five years now, I take comfort from that."

"She'll be in heaven now, Joe."

"I've got more to tell you, Violet Marsh, but I'm just about worn out now," Joe said and grinned at her, the effort of shaking off his sadness so clear to her. "So, I'm going to make up my little bed, the one I always used to sleep on over there by the window."

"No, I will sleep on that!"

"You're my guest and the best friend I ever had in my life, Vi. There's no way you're sleeping down there. The bed is for you, and you can rest assured I don't go wandering in the night," he said and grinned at her again, his allusion to her near misses of that nature made amusing in a way that only Joe Willis could make them amusing.

"Oh, how I've missed you! How I've missed you and the daft things you say!"

CHAPTER 17

"I hope nobody recognises me as the thief from yesterday," Violet said sheepishly, and Joe burst out laughing.

"Don't worry, I'll tell them I caught up with you, and I'm making you work hard now for the apple."

"It wouldn't surprise me at all if you actually say that."

"Just watch me," Joe said and winked, wheeling his cart through the street with Violet at his side.

She had insisted on helping him rather than staying in that comfortable bed. She rose just before four o'clock in the morning when he did, declaring that she was going to help him, that she was going to earn her keep. She walked through the streets with him to Covent Garden and back. It amazed her how alive the place was when it was still so early in the morning that it was dark. But there were fruit and vegetable merchants everywhere, all of them shouting and full of life as the smaller merchants and solo costermongers bought the produce that they hoped to sell that day.

When they passed a merchant selling flowers, Joe winked at the man and leaned forward to pluck out a single autumn rose. The man snorted with laughter; clearly, he knew the cheeky young man.

"Go on with you!" the man said and laughed, not charging a penny for the rose that Joe gave to Violet. "She's a pretty one, all right! Too good for a chopsey lad like you!"

"Thank you!" Joe called out, and they went on their way, wheeling the cart the mile back to the market at Piccadilly Circus.

Violet sniffed the rose now and again as they walked along, smiling and silently marvelling at how much her life had changed in just a day. Not to mention all the separate events which had finally brought her here, right back to Joe. Was it fate?

"What's up? You've gone quiet, Vi. I couldn't shut you up last night. Early morning getting to you, is it?"

"Ha! No, it isn't, I slept like a log!"

"What then?"

"I was just thinking about things. About how I got here… Like it was always a part of God's plan."

"I did tell you we'd be all right in the end, didn't I?"

"You were only eight years old, I thought you were making it up."

"O ye of little faith. God really does work in mysterious ways, don't he?" Joe smiled and winked at her just like he used to do when they were eight.

"What else did you have to tell me? Last night, you said there was much more to say; what was it?"

"Let's talk about it when we get back tonight," Joe said cautiously.

"No, let's talk about it now. Might as well have something to talk about while we're walking along."

"You're not going to give up, are you?"

"No," Violet said and grinned before sniffing the rose once more.

"All right, I'll carry on where I left off," Joe said, stoically pushing the cart but a little slower now as if he needed the time to get the entire story told. "So, I knew that your real ma had hidden you in Mayfair, that much Micah Turner had spilled before I legged it from the workhouse. Anyway, I used to look around the place a bit, I don't know why. I suppose I thought I might see a woman I recognised, one who looked like you and might really be your mother. Silly, I know, but that's what I did."

"It's not silly, Joe, it's kind and wonderful."

"Give over, you're embarrassing me," Joe said and chuckled before continuing. "Anyway, in the end, I started to ask old Bob about things. I mean, Oliver Daventry isn't really a common name, is it?"

"Did he know him?"

"He knew him to see; he'd heard about him. That's the way with the fine ladies and gents, though, isn't it? Everybody knows who they are, but they don't bother to know who we are, do they? Anyway, Bob told me about him. He knew where he lived, over in Mayfair. He had an idea that he had a daughter, but he didn't know if she was married or not. That was about it, really, for a few years. I didn't really know what to do with the little piece of information I had, and I didn't want somebody like Oliver Daventry, so desperate to keep you a secret that he chucked you in the workhouse, to know that I was poking around."

"You know where he lives, that's a start," Violet said.

"*Lived*, not *lives*. He's dead," Joe said without warning or ceremony.

"He's dead? When?"

"It was about a year and a half ago. I didn't know straight away; Bob told me. He remembered that I'd had an interest in the bloke when I was a kid, and I first started working for him. He said he thought I might like to know about it. Of course, that was as much as he did know, that the man was dead. So, I started asking around, feeling a bit braver, like I didn't have to be so cautious, you see. Anyway, I found out that the daughter, Esme Daventry, had inherited his house in Mayfair. I think she lived there anyway, the old man was a bit of a tartar and I think he wanted to keep a close eye on her after she had the baby out of wedlock and what have you. Anyway, not three months after the old man kicked the bucket, Esme Daventry married a man called Charles Lorimer. I even wandered about in Mayfair to have a look at the house, to see if I could have a look at Esme Daventry, or Lorimer, whatever her name is."

"Did you see her?"

"After about six weeks of trying, yes. And I was right, you look just like her. Shiny brown hair and those big brown eyes; there's no mistaking it."

"So, my real mother is just a few miles away?" Violet said, almost overwhelmed by a sense of wonder.

"Walking distance, Vi," Joe said and nodded. "Anyway, that was when I decided to come and find you, to tell you all about it. It was on a Sunday, the only day of the week that me and Bob didn't have work to do. And I reckoned it would be quiet enough in the workhouse that I might be able to sneak in and find you."

"That was very brave, what with Micah Turner trying to kill you and all."

"He wouldn't recognise me, I was fourteen by then, and I looked very different, didn't I? I mean *you* would recognise me, but we'd been friends. I doubt very much that Micah had studied me so closely that he'd have known me six years later."

"So, you actually went in?"

"I did. That's when I discovered that you'd not long disappeared. I was creeping about the place, and I found a woman that I think you described to me last night. Millie, wasn't it? A bedraggled woman with the madness on her. I recognised it straight away, but I chanced my arm and asked about you. Well, her eyes lit up, and she smiled from ear to ear. She said you'd run away in the middle of the night. She said that you wanted to take her with you, but I suppose that was just the madness talking."

"No, I *did* want to take her with me. I don't know what I would have done with her once we were out on the streets, but I couldn't bear to leave her there. But she wouldn't come, Joe. She said it was her life, that she'd die there." Violet shuddered, remembering those last moments in Millie's company and the shell of a woman that she had become.

"I was lost then, Vi. I knew something must've happened in that place, something which made you run. I asked the woman where you'd gone, but she just grinned at me and said that you were probably dead by now."

"Oh, dear, poor Millie," Violet said sadly.

"Yes, poor Millie. And poor me!" Joe pulled a face. "I thought you were dead, Vi!"

"It's something of a miracle that we found each other again, isn't it?"

"Yes, I suppose it is."

"And now I know everything, that you risked your life sneaking back into the workhouse to tell me. We're right here, with everything known."

"We *are* right here, Violet." He stopped for a moment, setting the cart down in the middle of the road and scratching his head.

"What is it?"

"I'm going to say something, Vi, and you can take it or leave it," he began and smiled. "I suppose as soon as I realised that old Oliver Daventry was dead, I had this idea of putting you and your ma back together again. I mean, she only lost you because he took you, didn't she? She never gave you away, did she? The fact is that you were stolen, and she didn't know where he'd put you. So, what with him being dead and all, maybe she would be pleased to see you. Maybe she'd want you back now."

"Do you really think so?" Violet asked and felt excited and afraid all at once. "I can't even remember what she looked like, Joe. I just remember holding her hand, feeling safe and loved in my little blue dress with the cream bow. Everybody said I was making it up, that nobody would put a fine dress on somebody like me. But I was right, wasn't I?"

"You were right, Violet. Do you want to see her?"

"I don't know. I mean, I *do* want to see her. I want to see her with all my heart, but won't she be ashamed of me? Would she take one look at the girl who grew up in a workhouse and shared a room with a prostitute and be glad that her father stole me away?"

"You're missing the point, Vi!" Joe said, and started to laugh. "The very reason that you grew up in a workhouse and had to share a room with a prostitute was *because* of her father stealing you away from her. If he hadn't, you might have managed quite nicely living with the old duck in Mayfair without old Oliver Daventry ever knowing you existed. And then, when he died, I've no doubt that Esme would have come for you."

"When you put it like that, I really would like to see her."

"All right then, well, I've got a plan. It's a plan I came up with before I came looking for you at the workhouse. As soon as old Oliver kicked the bucket, it sort of popped into my head. Do you want to hear it?"

"Yes, please."

"Well, I think you should try and get a job at the Lorimer house. See if you can get a position as a scullery maid or something, you must've learned how to do all that sort of thing in the workhouse, didn't you?"

"I did, but do you think she really would employ me?"

"In a big house like that, Vi, she wouldn't even see you. No, it's the housekeeper there that you'll have to impress because in the big houses, they're the ones who do the hiring and the firing. We'll work a really good tale out between us, and you're much more presentable than most, I reckon."

"Thank you," Violet said and grinned. "That was almost a compliment, Joe."

"I've always been a fast-talker, haven't I?" He laughed. "Right, let's get going with this cart before its dark, and all my customers have gone back home again. I can't stand here all day, nattering, can I? We can work out the details as the day goes on, that is if you want to stay out with me in the market. You can go back to the room if you want, of course."

"I wouldn't dream of it. I want to hear your plan, all of it."

CHAPTER 18

"Long time no see, Vi!" Joe said, grinning at her.

"What are you talking about? I was here yesterday!" Violet said and laughed. "Mrs Barton wants some more of them apples of yours; she's making a pie for some fancy meal tonight, apparently."

"I'll say one thing for your new job with the Lorimers; I'm doing a roaring trade in fruit and veg!" Joe said and started to put the best of his apples into Violet's wicker basket. "So, how's it going there?"

"Same as it was yesterday, Joe," Violet said, enjoying teasing him.

She had managed to secure a job in the Lorimer house with surprising ease. The housekeeper was a nice woman but very precise, and she liked Violet immediately. Violet had been more or less honest, as Joe had advised that it would be easiest to stick to her story if she was. He'd bought her a dress to wear, a very nice and respectable dress in a dark grey fabric. It was a sturdy work dress with long sleeves and a high neck, the very thing to present herself at the servants' entrance of a fine house. Joe had said that it would do her well to look the part, and so it had.

There was something else, though, which seemed to draw the housekeeper to her. Whether she realised it or not, her new scullery maid reminded her of somebody. Mrs Barton hadn't said it out loud, but Violet saw her looking at her from time to time, and she knew that the housekeeper was trying to place her.

"Well, that's not very informative, is it?" Joe said, still putting apples into the basket. "Stop me when it's too many, won't you?"

"It's already too many, Joe. She only wants eight!"

"You might have said something," he said and chuckled as he removed four apples from the basket, leaving exactly eight.

"Sorry," Violet was giggling.

"So, I take it you haven't set eyes on your ma," he said, lowering his voice to a whisper.

"No, not once. Being below stairs, I don't even get to look out of the windows at the front, so I can't watch out for her coming and going in the carriage and what have you. I haven't seen Mr Lorimer either, but the other servants speak very highly of them both. Apparently, they're very fair, and I suppose that's true if my wages are anything to go by. It's the first time in my life that I've have had any coins saved, let's put it that way."

"Well, it might take a bit of a while, but you might find that you'll work your way above stairs, so to speak. I mean working as a maid in the main part of the house, that type of thing. You'd definitely cross paths with Esme then, surely."

"Well, I've only been there a few weeks, so I'm not expecting miracles yet. But I do work hard, Joe, and I know Mrs Barton is happy with me. She even said it once or twice."

"Then I reckon you're well on your way. As long as she keeps letting you out to come for the groceries and what have you. As long as I still see you now and again, Violet Marsh!"

"After all these years, Joe, I'm not going to be parted from you again," Violet said and meant it. She could see that Joe knew that she meant it too, for his blue eyes seemed a little glassy with emotion.

"Go on with you, then, back to the big house!" he said, pulling a face and trying to hide his momentary softness. "You don't want to go getting the sack now, do you?"

"Will you start getting some water heated on the stove, Violet?" Mrs Barton asked some days later. "Ivy's upstairs stripping the beds, and it'll be nice to get them washed and out on the line whilst the sun is still out. Although, I don't doubt it will rain again later," Mrs Barton went on and sighed, but even so, she smiled.

"Yes, Mrs Barton," Violet said and immediately went to the cupboard in which the large water heating pan was kept.

As Violet went about her business, realising that she rather enjoyed her job in the Lorimer household, there was suddenly quite a commotion. Only Mrs Barton and Violet were in the large kitchen, for the cook was in her quarters having some tea and a slice of pound cake as she always did after her exertions with the morning's breakfast.

"Oh, Mrs Barton, It's Ivy!" Another of the maids who worked above stairs came dashing into the kitchen, her face pale, her expression one of panic.

"My goodness, what's happened?" Mrs Barton asked, a look of great concern on her face.

"She tripped on the upstairs landing, Mrs Barton, and she's twisted her ankle terribly. I don't know if it's broken or not, but she can't even stand," the maid looked tearful.

"All right, my dear, go and find two of the footmen and direct them upstairs; they'll need to carry the poor child down if she is hurt," Mrs Barton said, remaining calm and efficient despite her obvious concern. "You come with me, Violet. At least we can help her off the landing and into one of the guest bedrooms out of the way. We don't want to leave her on the landing in such a state, do we?"

"Of course, Mrs Barton," Violet said, and hurried out of the kitchen and along to the servants' back staircase, following along in the housekeeper's wake.

For a woman in her fifties, Mrs Barton was surprisingly nimble, climbing the stairs so quickly that Violet almost struggled to keep up with her. They climbed two flights, and when they came off the little landing and into the main part of the house, Violet's mouth fell open. They were in a beautifully wide corridor, a rich red and soft looking carpet runner travelled the full length. The walls were painted cream, and there were real gas lights fixed to the walls. They weren't lit, of course, but Violet had never seen such things before in her life. This really was a very fine house.

Her attention was sharply drawn away from the fixtures and fittings when she heard Ivy whimpering. She was on the floor, leaning against a closed door, tears rolling down her face. She was pale, and she looked to be in terrible pain, but Violet quickly crouched down by her side and took her hand.

"It's all right, Ivy. It's going to be all right, my dear," Violet said soothingly.

"That's right, Ivy," Mrs Barton said, not crouching down but placing a comforting hand on the top of Ivy's head. "The footmen are coming, and they're going to carry you downstairs. Now, don't you worry, my sweet, I'll send for the doctor immediately."

"Oh, my goodness, what on earth has happened?" The moment Violet heard the voice, she felt certain she knew who had spoken. It was a cultured voice, a beautifully clear, soft, wonderful voice. It could be none other than Esme Lorimer, her mother.

"Forgive me, ma'am, but young Ivy here has taken a dreadful tumble. Her ankle's twisted, perhaps even broken, and she is unable to walk on it. I've sent for two of the footmen to come and carry her down the stairs. Perhaps she could be carried down the main stairs, ma'am, it being wider and safer for the footmen to take her that way?"

"Oh, yes, of course, Mrs Barton. Oh, yes, she must be taken down most carefully." Violet hardly dared to look up, worried that she would simply dissolve when she set eyes on her mother at last. "Dear Ivy, are you in dreadful pain?" she continued to speak, directing her words to the distressed young maid.

"Yes, ma'am, it hurts terribly," Ivy said, her voice trembling.

"You mustn't worry, child, the doctor will be here as soon as possible." She paused for a moment and then addressed

Mrs Barton. "You will send for the doctor right away, won't you? Send one of the footmen for him and do say that I have asked for him most particularly, that I would be pleased if he would come immediately. Oh, if only Charles were here, he'd know what to do."

"Yes, ma'am, you're very kind," Mrs Barton said with warmth and respect. "Ah, here they come now," Mrs Barton went on, sounding relieved when she heard the footsteps on the servants' staircase.

In no time at all, two strong-looking young men had carefully lifted Ivy between them and were taking her down the main stairs in a gentle and respectful manner.

"I'll go down and make Ivy comfortable." Mrs Barton looked at Violet. "Violet, my dear, would you be so kind as to finish stripping the beds. I don't think poor Ivy will have got as far as making a start on it."

"Of course, Mrs Barton," Violet said, and finally raised her head; she had to, she would look far too conspicuous if she didn't.

"Thank you, child. Just bring the sheets and what have you downstairs when you've removed them. Oh, and please do take care, my dear, especially on the stairs." Mrs Barton turned to look at their mistress. "Forgive me, ma'am, I think this has left me a little shaken."

"Well, see that you take care of yourself, Mrs Barton.

Perhaps a brandy or something for the shock once you have Ivy settled?"

"You're very good, ma'am," Mrs Barton said, and then bowed her head respectfully before hurrying away along the corridor and back down the servants' staircase.

The moment had finally come; Violet was alone on the landing with her very own mother. She didn't know where to look, or even if it was acceptable for her to look directly at her mistress. These were the things that Mrs Barton would have taught her long in advance of her being promoted to work above stairs rather than below. But without that training, she felt lost at sea.

"Your name is Violet?" Esme Lorimer asked, studying her now. "What is your surname, my dear?"

"Marsh, ma'am. My name is Violet Marsh."

"And your mother? Is she still living?"

"I am afraid I never met my mother, ma'am. I was raised in the workhouse in Lambeth. I believe I was there from the time I was a small child, not yet three years old. I was sent there as an orphan." Violet's heart was pounding harder still.

"An orphan? But who placed you there?" Esme Lorimer seemed unable to take her eyes off Violet. She was studying her in every detail, and Violet was doing the same. After all these years, she was finally with the woman who had held her hand and walked her through the park.

She was finally with her mother, and she'd never been more afraid of rejection in her whole life.

"I didn't know until very recently, ma'am. I escaped at fourteen, and I didn't discover until I was fifteen the name of the man who had me placed in the workhouse."

"You are fifteen?"

"Yes."

"And how did you discover the name of the man who placed you in the workhouse?" Her eyes were shining, and Violet wondered if Esme Lorimer was going to cry.

"A boy I grew up in the workhouse with, a boy called Joe Willis, found it out seven years ago, but his life was threatened, and he had to escape before he could tell me what he learned. He only got as far as telling me that there was some secret concerning me."

"That being who you really were?" Tears were now streaming down Esme's face, and Violet knew that she knew exactly who stood before her.

"Yes," she said, holding back her own emotion.

"Who put you in the workhouse, Violet?" Esme's voice was trembling.

"A man called Oliver Daventry. He had been paying the Master of the workhouse, Micah Turner, to hide me there and keep his silence. I believe I was his granddaughter, and that he was ashamed of my existence," Violet said, her own voice cracking as her tears fell. "But I was his granddaughter, how could he do that?"

"I knew it was you. I knew you were my Violet." Esme was shaking with emotion as the two stood staring at one another.

"My grandfather arranged for me to be taken from my bed when I was staying with the elderly lady in Mayfair. That's as much as I know about my life before the workhouse."

"My poor little Violet. My only child locked away in the workhouse. Can you ever forgive me?"

"It wasn't your fault, ma'am. Oliver Daventry decided I couldn't be with you; it was his fault. As soon as I found you, I came to work here in the hope that you might see me one day and know me for who I am."

"My daughter," Esme whimpered, then took Violet into her arms and held her tightly.

"Oh, I remember you. I remember your touch," Violet said, almost swept away by the tide of emotions. "I remember walking through the park with you, holding your hand. It was all I could remember when I was in the workhouse. Everybody laughed at me. They all said that a wretch like me would never have worn a pretty blue dress made of fine silk with a cream bow."

"You remember it? You remember that little dress?"

"Yes. I remember it so clearly. I just couldn't remember your face or if I'd ever really had a mother. They tried to convince me that I was the unwanted child of a prostitute who just abandoned me on the steps of the workhouse."

"I would never have given you up willingly. My father knew that the moment he discovered the truth about you. I told him I would never let you go, and so he stole you. He always pleaded his innocence, but I knew it was him. I knew, and I never forgave him. It was just one more thing I could never forgive him for."

"You're not angry with me for coming here? I mean, I never wanted to embarrass you, and I shan't say a word to anybody. I just wanted to see you, to see your face and know that you didn't want to abandon me."

"I could never be angry with you. I'm so grateful to your little friend, the clever boy who found everything out and brought you back to me." Esme broke their embrace but held tightly to Violet's upper arms, studying her and smiling through her tears. "My goodness, you are so beautiful."

"So are you, ma'am."

"Not ma'am, *Mama*."

"But don't you mind? I mean, you're so beautiful and fine, and I'm so rough. I've gone through things I would be ashamed to tell you about."

"You mustn't be ashamed, not of anything. I have learned in my life that shame is a dreadful, wicked thing. It is a manmade thing designed by others to eat us from the inside out. You must discard it, Violet."

"I'll try." Violet paused for a moment, trying to find more courage. "Ma'am…Mama, what was my name when I was a baby? What did you call me?"

"Violet. I named you Violet Lorimer."

"Lorimer? But surely, that is your married name now?" Violet was confused.

"I have so much to tell you. Come, we cannot do that here on the landing. Come to my bedroom, and we'll talk over some tea."

"Oh, but I promised to bring down the sheets for Mrs Barton."

"Don't worry about that. I'll go down to Mrs Barton now and explain. The sheets can easily wait until another day when the maids aren't so busy with poor Ivy. Come, let me settle you in my room first."

CHAPTER 19

Her mother's rooms were large and beautifully decorated. The walls were covered with wallpaper, a delicate striped design with interwoven flowers. There was a white wooden table with two chairs set against it. The table's legs were intricately carved, and her mother had settled her there before dashing away.

Violet wondered what she would tell Mrs Barton. After all, she could hardly say that the illegitimate child she had given birth to fifteen years before had been working in the house as a scullery maid. And yet, Esme hadn't looked at all worried or furtive, only pleased to have her daughter back.

Everything seemed to be moving so fast. She felt guilty to be grateful that poor Ivy had twisted her ankle, but it had been the catalyst that had brought mother and daughter together again. Without it, she might not have come face to face with her mother for years. It was like Joe had said to her – God really does work in mysterious ways.

Nonetheless, Violet couldn't help but wonder what would happen next. And what of her mother's husband? Surely, he would know nothing of her existence. Surely, her mother couldn't risk telling him for fear of what he would do.

It was almost too much. There was too much to think about and far too much to hope for. Violet felt alive and exhausted all at once and was glad she was now sitting down at least; out on the landing, she had felt herself almost on the point of fainting.

"Here we are," her mother said brightly when she returned to the room. She was carrying a tray of tea herself, with no maid to help her. "Mrs Barton and the girls are so busy with Ivy, I didn't like to add to things," she went on by way of explanation.

"Is Ivy all right?" Violet asked, still feeling awkward as if she really ought only to speak when spoken to.

"The doctor is with her. He says the ankle isn't broken, but it is badly sprained. The poor thing will need to rest it for a good long while."

"I ought to help Mrs Barton. She'll be wondering where I am."

"She knows where you are," Esme said, and Violet had the greatest sense that Mrs Barton not only knew *where* she was, but *who* she was too. "We have much to talk about, you mustn't worry about anything else."

"Yes, ma'am. *Mama*," she said shyly; this was going to take some getting used to. She wished Joe could be right there with her.

"Let me pour you some tea. Then, I have something to show you," Esme said, her voice so gentle, so maternal, that Violet began to feel emotional again. She watched as her mother poured them both tea and added a little milk to each cup from a pretty floral jug. "There, take a sip, you look pale and exhausted."

"Thank you," Violet said and took a sip.

Esme left her own tea and crossed the room to a beautiful wide oak chest of drawers. She opened the very top drawer and reached inside. She drew out a little parcel wrapped in delicate tissue paper and walked back across the room. Violet watched as she sat down, the parcel on her lap. As Esme untied the ribbon around the tissue paper, Violet held her breath; it was her dress. It was her little blue silk dress with the cream bow. It was exactly as she remembered it being.

"That's the little dress I was wearing. It's just how I remembered it," Violet said and began to cry again. Her mother took a pretty embroidered handkerchief from the sleeve of her dress and handed it to her.

"All I had left of you was this dress. My father got rid of everything else, but Emily Marlow, the kind lady who tried to help me keep you a secret, still had this. When I realised that I would never find you, she gave it to me as a keepsake."

"She sounds like a kind woman."

"The kindest. She was my mother's governess when she was a girl, and she knew that my mother, had she been alive, would have done anything to help keep you with me. She was a gentle soul. My father, on the other hand, was a different matter. The truth is, had he not been so determined to rule my life, you would never have been born out of wedlock, and I would never have had to hide you away."

"I don't understand."

"Your father, Violet, well, I loved him with all my heart. I loved him so much that I knew I would never love another man my whole life. But your grandfather had other plans for me, and marrying the man I loved wasn't a part of that."

"He wanted you to marry somebody else?"

"Yes, a man I couldn't abide. I refused, of course, and my father's punishment was to keep me away from Charles. Only I couldn't stay away from him; my heart was broken. When I discovered I was expecting you, it was the happiest day of my life. I knew it wouldn't be easy, but I was never going to let you go."

"And my father? Did he see me?"

"Yes, he did. That's how you were discovered. My father suspected me of still seeing Charles, so he had him followed. Followed all the way to Emily Marlow's house. It wasn't long before they saw me taking you out to the park. And then you were gone. One night, my father had someone sneak into Emily's home and take you."

"You must have been…"

"Heartbroken, yes. My father tore me to pieces with his words, calling me all sorts of awful names, things I could never repeat. But when I accused him of stealing you, he denied all knowledge. It was ridiculous, but he kept his secret and took it to the grave with him. If only we had run sooner."

"Run?"

"When you were almost three, Charles and I decided to elope. We decided to be married and live without my father's support. Charles was a gentleman, but not a wealthy man. That was my father's only objection to him." She dabbed at the corner of her eye with slim, soft fingers. "We were too late."

"You could still have married."

"My father kept me a prisoner in this house for more than a decade after you went. I never saw Charles again until after my father died. He said he'd tried so many times, but he couldn't get past my father."

"So, my father is still alive?"

"He's alive," Esme said and reached for her hand. "After my father died, Charles and I were married. I am married to your father, Violet."

"Of course. Violet Lorimer!"

"Yes, you are Violet Lorimer."

"Will he want to see me? Will my father be pleased to see me as you are pleased?"

"Oh, he will. He has searched for you for so many years. He went to every orphanage in London, but there was no sign of you. I don't think either one of us would imagine so tiny a child being placed in a workhouse. We thought my father had had you sent out of London, maybe even out of the country. We thought there was no hope of ever finding you again." She sighed and bowed her head. "My father was a rotten man. Even so, I could never have imagined he would have placed you in the workhouse. My poor child, how you must have suffered. But you must tell me it all, leave nothing out. I must know everything that happened to you."

"I don't know where to begin," Violet said, just as there came a gentle knock at the door.

Esme got to her feet and smiled encouragingly at Violet before reaching for the door handle. Violet knew it would be her father, and her heart began to pound again.

"Mrs Barton said you wanted to see me, my love. Is everything all right? Are you ill?" The voice was deep but gentle, the voice of her father.

"I am better than well, my dear Charles. I can hardly believe it, but she is here. She is found!"

"She is found. You mean…? You mean our little girl?" His voice cracked instantly with emotion, and he gently pushed his way into the room.

He was tall, and his brown hair was flecked with thick greys. His eyes were kindly, and he stood looking at her, tears running down his face. Violet knew she had seen him before. Her father was the kind gentleman who had saved her from the taunting drunk when she had been collecting pure by the Vauxhall Pleasure Gardens. The man who had given her a few coins and looked upon her with such sadness. And at the moment that she recognised him, she could see that he recognised her too.

CHAPTER 20

"Are you looking forward to tea, Violet?" her mother asked as she helped to pin up her hair. She always insisted on doing that herself; she'd missed out on too much of her child's life already.

"Yes, very much. I just hope I do everything right," Violet said, still nervous after almost a year of living with her parents.

"You always do, and what does it matter if you don't?" her mother said and kissed the top of her head. "Oh, how beautiful you are. I can hardly believe my little girl is already sixteen years old!"

"What is the Lawlor family like, Mama? Do they know all about me? About my past?" Violet asked, feeling the familiar twitch of nerves in her stomach.

"They know about you, my sweet because you have never done anything wrong. I don't need to hide you or what happened. If that was something that the Lawlor family was unable to manage, they wouldn't be in my life in the first place. Violet, you will find that I don't have many friends, but the ones I do have are good and strong. Jennifer Lawlor is an old friend of mine, one who has been a great comfort to me in the past."

"Like Joe was to me?"

"Yes, like Joe was to you," her mother said, but Violet could hear the catch of hesitation in her voice. Worse still, it wasn't the first time she'd heard it.

It had been a wonderful year at the house in Mayfair, in the heart of a small but extraordinarily loving family. At first, her mother didn't seem to mind her wandering off to Piccadilly Circus to see Joe as he worked at his cart, and it had never occurred to Violet that she ever would. After all, without Joe, Esme Lorimer's daughter would never have been returned to her.

However, of late, Violet had sensed a change. It wasn't much, not something that anybody else might have noticed, but Violet had. Mother and daughter had made a great study of one another. Making up for lost time, and she felt she knew her well now, as well as she might have known her had they never been parted, perhaps even better for the determined study and time spent together. She even believed she knew what it was that perturbed her mother now. Violet was a young woman, sixteen years old and of an age where her thoughts turned to the man she might marry one day. She tried not to think about it, for it hurt too much, but she had a suspicion that her mother wanted better for her.

It wasn't an unusual concept for a mother to think that way, of course, it wasn't, but Violet knew that there wasn't a finer young man in all the world than Joe Willis. Violet didn't want it to build a wall between mother and daughter, but she was silently determined never to let go of Joe. She loved him; she'd loved him all her life. She'd loved him since she was a child, and now that love had changed into something else altogether, something her mother of all people ought to have understood.

Charles Lorimer was a different kettle of fish, and Violet was glad of it. His easy relationship with Joe and his obvious care for the young man soothed Violet whenever she thought of it. He took a great interest in him, marvelling at the young man's ingenuity and work ethic when he purchased two more carts to rent out. He now owned six, taking a passive income from the other five. He was getting money behind him and had even gone as far as opening a bank account with the help of her father. Charles Lorimer was named administrator on the account, something the bank had insisted upon, given Joe's young age and uncertain background. Charles had even made provision to continue Joe's education, just as Violet's own was continuing. He could see great promise in the young man, and it made it somehow clearer to Violet that her mother didn't see things the same way.

"I think you're going to enjoy this afternoon, my dear. Jennifer has a rather wonderful son. He's a little older than you, and his name is Henry. He's been away studying, but he'll be back for the entire summer. I'm sure he would be very grateful for a friend in Mayfair to attend dances with and what have you." As her mother spoke, Violet's heart sank.

"Forgive me, Mama, but may I be excused from afternoon tea?" Violet said, knowing that her mother would much prefer her to turn her attention to Henry Lawlor than Joe.

"Excused, my sweet? But why? Are you unwell?"

"No, I'm not unwell, Mama," Violet said and felt so sad that her eyes filled with tears. "I'm not unwell. I'm just sad, and I want to go and see Joe."

"Joe Willis? But why? We're supposed to be having afternoon tea!" Her voice was gentle, but her disappointment was clear.

"Because I'm never going to love Henry Lawlor, and I think that's what you want."

"You've never met him, Violet. Can you not just have afternoon tea with him and give him a chance?"

"No," Violet said and dashed out of the room.

She didn't want to argue with her mother, she loved her so much. This was the only thing that stood between them, the only stumbling block. But she couldn't bear the idea of the two of them at loggerheads, no more than she could bear the idea of living her life without Joe. Even when everything was going right, something had to go wrong, didn't it?

By the time she reached the bottom of the stairs, Violet was in floods of tears. She could hear her mother hurrying along behind her, but she didn't want to speak to her. She wanted to get away, to find her cloak, put it on, and dash out of the door. She didn't want to meet Henry Lawlor, however nice he might be. She just wanted to run and run until she reached Piccadilly Circus and Joe.

At that moment, however, her father came out of the drawing room and stood looking at his wife and daughter with some confusion.

"I could hear running," he said gently. "What's the matter? Are you both all right?"

"We are fine, Charles," Esme said, continuing to hurry down the stairs and taking advantage of the fact that Violet was now stationary in the entrance hall. "Violet is just a little upset," she went on and sounded somewhat sheepish.

"I can see," Charles said gently. "Come on into the drawing room, Violet, let's see if we can't get to the bottom of things," he went on, ushering her into the drawing room. "Now then, sit yourself down, Violet." Charles was smiling at her, so kind and fatherly as always. "What's the matter, my dear girl?"

"I think I tried to push her too hard, Charles. I just thought that Henry Lawlor... Well, he's back for the summer, and his parents are such fine people," Esme said, speaking hurriedly when it seemed Violet would remain silent.

"Ah, so you've been meddling, my love," Charles said and started to laugh.

"She's my daughter, Charles, I hardly think it's meddling," her mother said, but as much as she was trying to defend herself, Violet could see the regret in her beautiful eyes, and it made her heart ache. "I'm sorry, my dear, I really am. Henry is a nice young man, and I thought you might like him too."

"Mama, I have no doubt he's a nice man. I have no doubt I would like him." She shrugged and quickly dried her face with her handkerchief. "But I'll never love him. I know I'll never love him."

"But how do you know that?" her mother persisted.

"Because I'm already in love, Mama. I love Joe, I always have. He's the only man I could ever love."

"But you are both so young. You never know how much you're going to change in the coming years. You might find that Joe isn't the man you want."

"No, I won't," Violet spoke firmly. She did not look at her father in case she saw his agreement with her mother.

"Joe is a very fine young man, and he has been so brave, but he… well…" Her mother's voice trailed away to nothing.

"He's *what*, Esme?" Charles asked, and his voice was every bit as firm as Violet's had been. "Shall I finish that sentence for you, my love?" he went on. "I think you're trying to say that Joe isn't a wealthy young man." As Violet studied her father's face, she could see both hurt and disappointment there.

"I'm so sorry, I just wanted the best for her. I just want the best," Esme said and began to cry.

"You can't decide for another person, Esme. And if you stop and think about what you're saying for a moment, you might see the similarity in everything your father said to you about me. He would have liked me well enough, as you like Joe, but he didn't think I was good enough because I wasn't wealthy. And did he not try exactly the same tactics? Did he not tell you that you would change soon, that you were too young to know your own mind and heart? No, I won't have my daughter suffer as you did, as I did," Charles said, and his eyes were shining with emotion.

"Oh, my goodness, oh, my goodness," Esme said as her head dropped, and she covered her face with her hands. "I cannot believe I have done just the same thing."

"It wasn't the same thing, Mama," Violet said and moved along the couch to sit right beside her. "I do understand, it must be so strange for you to think that I would love a young man who was raised in the workhouse, but you forget that I was raised in the workhouse, too. My history is his history; he knows me, and I know him. That is how I can tell you with confidence that Joe will marry me one day, that he loves me, even though he's never spoken the words. That is how well I know him, how deep our love is. Please, don't ask me to let go of him, Mama, because I never shall."

"Nor should you, my love," Esme said and was sobbing now. "Oh, what have I become? How have I forgotten so easily how I felt when I was young? I knew I loved your father, just as you know that you love Joe. Please forgive me, Violet, please forgive me."

"I don't need to forgive you for caring about me, Mama," Violet said tearfully as she put her arms around her mother's shoulders. "I don't need to forgive you for loving me so much, do I? All I need to do is love you in return. Life isn't so simple, is it?"

"You're a good girl, Violet," Charles said and sat down on the other side of her, and she felt the safety and warmth of the love and care of her doting parents.

"I can't wait to give your father his money back, Vi," Joe said as they walked along the wide sunlit streets of Mayfair. "Not that I'm not grateful, but I just want to see his face. He'll be so pleased that I'm turning a good profit now."

"I know he will. He'll be so proud of you, Joe." Violet looked over her shoulder. "I'm going to have to help Miss Butterworth out with the children; they're leading her a merry dance, look. They're trying to cajole her into the park."

"Let's go into the park then. Clara and William just want to play for a while, and we're early, so where's the harm?" He laughed and turned her towards the park. The governess, seeing the change in direction, looked relieved.

"You're a good father, Joe. The children love you so much." And it was true, Clara, six, and William, just four, were such happy, loving children. Even though their father worked so hard, he still made time for them. He still made time for his beautiful wife.

"You're a good mother!" he said, making her laugh. Joe had changed a little, but not too much. He would never forget his past, his roots, and rather than feeling ashamed, he was always proud of the mother who had raised him to be a good boy with a kind heart and a ready wit.

"I love you," Violet said, and her eyes filled with tears as they always did when she thought about their journey through life.

"I love you. I always did." He turned her to face him and

kissed her right there in the park. Clara, the only witness to the secret display, squealed with delight.

Joe and Violet had married when they were eighteen years old. It had been Charles' only condition, and they had both agreed to wait, even though eighteen was still considered so young in their new social circles. But they didn't care; they were in love, and they both knew it was forever. There had never been any sense in putting it off.

In eight years of marriage, so much had changed. Joe had sold his costermonger business and all his carts, adding the money to his savings in hopes of leasing a small shop. Seeing his determination, Charles had given him some money so that he might open two shops, and Joe had taken it gratefully.

However, Joe being Joe, he had made the two little shops work well for him, and soon two shops became four, and then five. He had a growing reputation in the retail industry, and Willis' Department Stores, selling everything from clothing to furniture, was becoming a household name.

The young couple had a nice house and wanted for nothing, and the children had never known a day's hardship, even though both parents were determined they should know that life was not always so easy for others.

Joe had made such a success of things that he was able to return Charles Lorimer's original loan with the proper interest, and Violet could see just how proud that made him. Her mother and father would be proud of him, too, knowing now that they could not have given their daughter away to a better man.

Violet's father had been able to pull a few strings, and get Micah Turner ousted from the workhouse and arrested. Someone new had been put in charge – Violet wasn't sure who – but at least that awful man was no longer in a position of power. Violet could feel a small sense of redemption, knowing she had saved countless girls from his vile grasp.

"Vera Packham had unexpectedly left the workhouse only a couple of weeks after Violet had run away. Violet never saw her again. As she matured, Violet came to see that Vera had been a victim too - just like all the other girls – to Mr Turner's cruelty, but Violet hoped and prayed that Vera found peace within herself, and let go of all the bitterness and cruelty."

Millie had been taken to Cane Hill, and Violet had made sure to visit her every week. Miraculously, she gradually started to show signs of improvement. Violet's constant prayers and her kindness and patience during each of her visits certainly had something to do with Millie's recovery. It had been very slow, but after two years, Millie was recovered enough to be allowed to move out of Cane Hill, and Joe had been able to employ her in one of his shops. The emotional scars that her experiences in the workhouse might never truly fade, but by the grace of God and the kindness of others, she was taking control of her life again. Violet had even been the matron of honour at Millie's wedding; she had married a respectable young gentleman who was also a clerk at the shop.

After the first year of living once again with her family, Violet had sought out Lily too. It had taken her that long to finally feel at peace enough to forgive Lily for her cruelty and be ready to face her – alas, she had been too late. She had found out by asking around that Lily had passed away, only a couple of months after Violet and her had so violently parted ways. Violet had made sure a small gravestone in their local church had been placed there for Lily, and she visited it often, keeping Lily in her prayers even now, alongside all other women who were trapped in such heinous conditions.

"Mind this, Clara Willis!" Joe called out, tapping the side of his nose and grinning at his daughter. "She was my wife before she was your mama, you know!" He was every bit the cheeky tease he'd always been, and his daughter giggled with amusement. However, being her father's daughter, Clara had no intention of minding her business, and so she simply grinned and stared at them.

"It's your own fault, Joe! She's just like you." Violet leaned against him as they began to walk again.

"You think I'm nosey?"

"No, not nosey, just cheeky. Clara is just as cheeky as you were at that age."

"I remember so clearly being six years old, Vi. I wonder if our own children will be able to do the same."

"Why?"

"Well, I think we remember because the harshness of our lives made it hard to forget. I mean, look at them, they are everything children should be. They're carefree and happy, and it's all I could ever have wished for them."

"We certainly weren't carefree and happy at six. And yes, I remember it as clearly as you do. Perhaps you're right, perhaps the memory is sharper for the hardship. We were so old for our years, weren't we?"

"We didn't have a childhood." Joe looked suddenly sad.

"I know, but we had each other. Not for all of it, but when we were little, we had each other. I'll be happy to remember that fact for the rest of my life." A single tear ran down her cheek, and Joe gently wiped it away.

"So will I. I loved you then, and I love you now. I'll love you forever."

"And I'll love you forever too, Joe Willis."

"Come on, let's get to your ma's place before we're both sobbing like children!" Joe said and grinned before taking her hand and hurrying her through the park.

THANK YOU FOR CHOOSING A PUREREAD BOOK!

We hope you enjoyed the story, and as a way to thank you for choosing PureRead we'd like to send you this free book, and other fun reader rewards...

Click here for your free copy of Whitechapel Waif
PureRead.com/victorian

Thanks again for reading.
See you soon!

OTHER BOOKS BY JESS WEIR

If you enjoyed this story why not continue straight away with other books by the same Author?

The Coal Beggar Maid's Christmas

The Little London Nightingale

The Midwife's Dream

The Mill Daughter's Courage

The Orphan Pickpocket's Christmas

The Foundling's Despair

OUR GIFT TO YOU

AS A WAY TO SAY THANK YOU WE WOULD LOVE TO SEND YOU THIS BEAUTIFUL STORY FREE OF CHARGE.

Click here for your free copy of Whitechapel Waif

PureRead.com/victorian

At PureRead we publish books you can trust. Great tales without smut or swearing, but with all of the mystery and romance you expect from a great story.

Be the first to know when we release new books, take part in our fun competitions, and get surprise free books in your inbox by signing up to our free VIP Reader list.

As a welcome gift you'll receive the story of the Whitechapel Waif straight to your inbox...

Click here for your free copy of Whitechapel Waif

PureRead.com/victorian

Printed in Dunstable, United Kingdom